My Story

THE FALL OF THE BLADE

Sue Reid

SCHOLASTIC

For Alison and Rob

While the events described and some of the characters in this book may be based on actual historical events and real people, Isabelle is a fictional character, created by the author, and her story is a work of fiction.

Scholastic Children's Books
Euston House, 24 Eversholt Street,
London, NW1 1DB, UK
A division of Scholastic Ltd
London ~ New York ~ Toronto ~ Sydney ~ Auckland
Mexico City ~ New Delhi ~ Hong Kong

Published in the UK by Scholastic Ltd, 2010

ISBN 978 1407 11118 6

Printed and bound by CPI Bookmarque Ltd, Croydon, Surrey

2 4 6 8 10 9 7 5 3 1

Meudon, France 1792

Meudon, 30 July 1792

I have begun a diary. I am not going to tell anyone about it. I am not sure what Mama would think. She often says that we must be careful what we say and write now, but I will burst if I cannot ever say how I truly feel. This diary will have to do instead. I am writing it on the blank pages of one of my old schoolbooks. I keep it under the mattress. I wish I could think of a better place for it, but I don't think that anyone will find it there.

It is because of the Revolution that we have to be so careful. Papa says the Revolution was a fine thing and there was much that was wrong with France that needed to be put right, but I wish it would end!

If it doesn't Papa may carry out his threat and send us to live in our old château in Picardy. He says that it would be safer for us there than here but I would rather we stayed here. Papa likes the old château. He grew up in it, but we have never lived in it for long. I hope we never do. The few times I stayed there I was far too scared to sleep.

Meudon, 2 August 1792

I am glad I decided to keep a diary. I know that I will enjoy
writing in it. I think I should begin by telling you a little
about me. My name is Isabelle and I am the only daughter
of a marquis – though perhaps it would be more accurate
to say that I was *born* the daughter of a marquis. Our titles
were abolished by law after the Revolution began. So now
I am plain citizenness Isabelle! Our servants and friends
still address Papa as Monsieur le marquis though. It is
most confusing.

Meudon, 4 August 1792

Papa left for Paris again today. He doesn't go as often as he
did, and I'm glad, because I don't like it when he's gone. I feel
happier when he's here to look after us all. My big brother,
François, is at home all the time now. He had to leave
college when the authorities closed all the colleges down.

4

That was because of the Revolution too. François says they did it because people don't like aristocrats like us and are closing down or abolishing everything that reminds them of us. I wish François wouldn't say such things. It makes me feel uncomfortable.

I must tell you about my Papa. I am very proud of him. He is a deputy in the Assembly that governs France. He is clever and honest and I think the country is fortunate that he still wishes to serve it. Few noblemen do. Many of them think that things have gone too far and would like the King to have his powers restored to him. Not Papa, he says that the country needed to be reformed. The poor paid most of the taxes and it was most unfair. Before the Revolution our King – Louis XVI – ruled France with the help of his ministers. Everyone had to do exactly as the King wished. His power was absolute. But after the Revolution began he lost most of his power to the Assembly.

This is the third Assembly there has been since the Revolution began. That was three years ago, in 1789. Just think! It has been going on now for three years. Sometimes it feels as if it has been going on for ever. It began when a mob stormed the Bastille prison in Paris and let out all the prisoners. There were only seven of them, but some people said the rest must have been murdered or released before it fell. Each year now on the 14 July, the date the Bastille fell, a special fête is held to celebrate the beginning of the Revolution.

I was only ten then. No one told me about it, but I soon learnt what had happened. You couldn't help hearing about it. Our château was always full of people then and politics was all anyone ever talked about. They sounded so excited – talking about liberty and how things would be better in France for everyone, not just rich aristocrats like us. But after the Bastille fell a lot of our friends left the country. We have few visitors now – except M Le Blanc, my harp teacher, and M Brouquart, Papa's steward who manages our estates. But I don't count them.

I cannot imagine that we will ever emigrate. Papa thinks it is wrong to desert your country. I heard him say that many of the émigrés have joined the armies of our enemies – Austria and Prussia. (We are at war with Austria and Prussia.) That makes them traitors in Papa's mind. And I think it is wrong to fight against your own countrymen. Papa says that there are many people here in France who want to stir up civil war. He calls them "counter-revolutionaries" because they are against the Revolution. I suppose that makes François a counter-revolutionary, as he is against it too. But he only talks about how wrong the Revolution is. He doesn't stir anything up.

I am sure you can tell by what I have written that I am quite clever at finding things out. I am thirteen, but small for my age so people often don't notice me, and say things in front of me that otherwise they would not. And if they do there are lots of places here where I can hide, so I learn much that I wouldn't otherwise know.

Meudon, 7 August 1792

Marguerite's dog Bébé has had a litter of puppies. (Marguerite is our gardener's wife.) I am fond of her and sometimes I help her in her little garden.

The puppies are adorable. I sat and played with them for a long time. They clambered all over me. I hope Mama will let me have one. I have my eye on the one that was the first to climb on to my lap. He's the littlest of the litter and has the softest ears and such dark gentle eyes. I could hardly bear to put him down and when I tried to hand him back he took one of my fingers into his mouth and would not let go of it – as if he didn't want me to leave either. All the way though my harp lesson I was thinking about him – his dark eyes and soft ears. Perhaps that is why I played worse than usual. I am not musical like Mama. You should hear me sing! I don't think M Le Blanc noticed though. He spent much of my lesson staring out of the window and saying "good, very good" even when I made a mistake which I did about 100 times. Papa was home and he and M Le Blanc stood and talked for a long time. Their faces were very serious so when they were not looking I slipped behind the curtain to listen. But they spoke so low that I could not hear a single word.

Meudon, 8 August 1792: late

It is late, but I simply had to write. I am so happy. Mama has said I may have the puppy. I have been thinking and thinking what to call him and have decided to call him Wolf. François says it is a ridiculous name for a small puppy and that "petit chien" would suit him better. He is wrong. He has not seen Wolf's sire. He is huge! One day my little dog will grow to be just as big.

Meudon, 9 August 1792

I am sitting up in bed, writing. Wolf is curled up next to me. I have been playing with him, but he is asleep now. I'd like to sleep too, but I am trying to stay awake until Papa returns.

He left for Paris early this morning but promised to return by nightfall. It is dark now but he is still not back.

I am most anxious to see him. I gave him a letter for my friend Claire, which he promised to deliver for me. Claire is my closest friend, and last year I went to her elder sister's wedding. I have written to her several times since then, but have not had a single reply. I want to tell her about Wolf. Papa says she will probably be on their estate in the country, but I have already written to her there and she did not reply to that letter either.

The servants have lit all the candles. Papa should be home by now. He *promised* me he would be back by nightfall. What can have kept him in Paris so late?

Meudon, 10 August 1792: early morning

I have barely slept and am tired and frightened. My candle has long gone out, but I can see well enough now to write without it.

All night long bells have been ringing. I closed the windows to shut out the noise, but I can still hear them. And just now I heard a distant boom-boom – as if cannon have been fired. Something terrible must be happening in the city. But what? If only I knew.

The din woke both Wolfie and me. I got up straightaway. I forgot that Wolfie was on the bed and my poor little puppy slithered right off the bed on to the floor. He gave me a most reproachful look. I picked him up and put him back on the bed, before hastening to the window. Outside my chamber door I could hear anxious raised voices, and slippered feet pattering back and forth across the floor. Others had woken too. But I did not go out to them. I leaned out of the window to listen, the night air fresh on my face. Meudon, where we live, is on a hill, scarce a league from the city. My chamber faces north and when it is light I can see the towers and walls that encircle it. Just beyond the city is the hill where the village of Montmartre lies.

But in the dark, I could see nothing at all. I felt my heart flutter inside my chest. What had caused the alarm to be sounded? I rang the bell for Marie, and she brought me a candle. Her hands were trembling as she put it down on the table. I got back into bed but I didn't feel any better even with the candle lit, so I pulled on a shawl and went to find Mama. We huddled together on her bed while she stroked my hair to comfort me. I climbed in next to her because my feet were cold. It was almost light and Mama was fast asleep by the time I went back to bed. Outside my chamber now I can hear voices. The servants are up. It will soon be time for me to rise. I must be patient. But how can I be? I long for news. But I dread it too.

10

Later

There has been a battle in the city! That is why the bells were ringing last night. The King's own Swiss guards are being murdered by French National Guards – in the courtyard of the King's palace itself! Even those guards who have managed to escape from the palace are being hunted down and killed in the street by the mob.

I was sitting sewing with Mama when news of the battle was brought. I was so startled that I drove the needle into my thumb instead of into the handkerchief I was embroidering. The handkerchief is quite ruined, and blood has spotted my gown. Fortunately, in all the uproar Mama did not notice and Marie has put it in water to soak.

There are so many rumours flying about that it is hard to know what to believe. Some say that the King's Swiss guards started the battle by firing on the city's National Guards. Others insist that the National Guards fired first. Why anyone fired at all, we none of us know. François thinks the whole thing was plotted by the revolutionaries. But he would. I cannot stop worrying about Papa. He did not return last night. I pray that he is safe. Oh Papa, come home to us. Please.

No one can enter or leave the city. Pierre, one of our menservants, says the farmer was not able to take his wagon into the city this morning. His wagon was held up at the gates. All the barriers are closed and the guards refuse to let anyone in or out.

There is no news of the King and his family. We do not even know if they are alive or dead. The farmer dared not ask the guards for fear of being branded a royalist. It is dangerous to be thought a royalist now. But I heard Marie say to Annette that she trembles when she thinks what might have happened to them. I have been to our tiny chapel to light a candle for them – and for Papa, too, of course. Our priest was there, but he was on his knees and so deep in prayer that he did not hear me come in. Papa says the King is not to be trusted, but I cannot help feeling sorry for him and for his family. The Princess is the same age as me! I have been thinking about her and her little brother, who is the Dauphin and the King's heir. I used to wish I had been born a princess, but I cannot think of anything I'd like to be less now. It is not a good thing to have been born the daughter of an aristocrat either. Even though our titles and privileges have been abolished people still seem to hate us.

Meudon, 11 August 1792

A servant has brought a letter from Papa. He is safe! I am so relieved. I have hardly been able to eat for worrying. François thinks I was stupid to worry. He thinks that the deputies are responsible for what happened – and so they are probably the safest people in the kingdom. He must know that cannot be true. Papa would never consent to such a thing. The real power must lie elsewhere.

We still have had no news of the King. Papa said nothing about him in his letter. I lit another candle for him today.

Meudon, 12 August 1792

I want to talk to our priest, but he has disappeared. No one has seen him. François thinks he has gone into hiding. I asked François why he would do that. And then he told me something that has truly frightened me. It seems there has been much talk among the servants about France's enemies.

Gaspard, one of our servants, says you do not know who they are – they are not just the Prussians marching towards us. They are here, in our midst. "Are you saying that our priest is one of France's enemies?" I said to François indignantly. "How can you think so?"

François sighed, patiently – in that annoying way of his when he thinks I am being stupid. "I don't think that, of course I don't – but he may believe that others do. He may think he is in danger."

I was puzzled so he explained that priests had been asked to take an oath, to put their country first, before their allegiance to the Pope. How could anyone ask that of a priest! But even if they do refuse to take the oath, does that mean they will betray their country? I cannot believe that.

I have been thinking about François's words. They make me tremble. "Our enemies are here, in our midst." Are we *all* under suspicion now? It is too awful to think about.

Meudon, 13 August 1792

François and I have made a pact – to hide anyone who asks us to. I don't care if they are royalists or revolutionaries. François would rather they were royalists but he agrees that we should hide anyone who needs help. We may even need to find a safe place to hide ourselves. So we spent this afternoon in the park looking for good places to hide in. We went first to the ice house, and then we tried the stables. When the groom wasn't looking François climbed up into the hayloft, but I think they'd be sure to find you there, even if you do cover yourself with hay. Anyway, it was dusty which made him sneeze. "I have a much better place," I said. "Come with me." And I took him to my special hiding place. I'd never told him about it, even though he is my brother. I didn't want to tell him now, but we hadn't found anywhere else. I think it's the best place of any we've found. It's just a tree stump in the copse, but it is hollow inside and you can fit in easily. No one would see you there. I sit in it sometimes when I want to be alone to think. No one has ever found me. I climbed in to show him, but François was not impressed. He thinks it's too small for a grown man to hide in and that he'd do better climbing up a tree. He thinks the place we found next is best – but it's smelly. And it's stupid. How long can a man cling on to a rope while dangling down the well? But François says these are desperate times. We have tried to find secret hiding places inside the house too. I tap all the walls when no one is looking, to see if there is a secret chamber. But if there is one, I haven't found it.

Meudon, 15 August 1792

I am so glad that I began this diary. I can write anything I like in it – and no one ever needs to know. What would I do without it? And now I am gladder of it than ever. I have an important secret to confide. We have a fugitive hiding in our house. There. I can scarcely believe I have written that.

Even when we were searching for hiding places, I never truly thought we'd need to hide anyone. I felt quite excited at first, but now that I have had time to think I am scared. What if someone were to find him? What would happen to him? What would happen to *us*? We still do not know who he is or anything about him – except that he is wounded, so it is not hard to guess that he was in the battle. He is too weak to talk much at all.

It was I who found him! He was hiding in the copse. I was making my way to my secret tree stump when I nearly fell over him. He was hunched up by a tree nearby. I did not feel at all how I thought I would. I wanted to run away but my legs wouldn't move. We stared at each other. He is not very tall, so he could have hidden in my tree stump, but if he had I might not have found him. And he'd never have been able to crawl into it, or climb into the hayloft or hide in the well – not with that sword cut in his leg. It made me feel quite sick. It wasn't bleeding but the blood had soaked through the handkerchief he'd used to staunch it. And then I felt ashamed of myself. What had I to be afraid of? He was only a boy, like François. And it was he who was hiding – not me. I walked closer to him. I saw then that he was shivering, and it wasn't a cold morning.

"Don't be afraid," I said nervously. "I won't hurt you. I want to help you." I reached out and laid my hand on his forehead. He didn't try to stop me. It felt very hot. "How long have you been here?" I asked.

The boy licked his dry lips. "All night," he whispered. Then I asked his name but though I could see his lips move I could not hear what he was saying now. It seemed to be an effort for him to speak at all. I tried to think what to do. He could not stay there. He was ill. I had to tell Mama.

Mama came at once. She didn't ask me who he was, or why he was there, or where he'd come from, but immediately followed me to the copse and gently told him that we would look after him until he was quite better. I knew she would. I love Mama!

We smuggled him into the house when no one was around. He could hardly walk and had to lean heavily on François's shoulder, half hopping, half dragging his wounded leg. His face was pale and there were drops of sweat on his forehead. It must have hurt very much. Mama led the way, beckoning us in when the hall was empty. François murmured to me that he hoped no one had been watching from the windows. I wish he hadn't.

He is in Mama's chamber now. She had wanted to put him in the attic, but he would never have managed to climb another flight of stairs. I cannot imagine how he managed to walk all the way to Meudon. Mama has let Annette, her waiting woman, into the secret, but has told us not to breathe a word to anyone else. The fewer people who knew that we had a wounded boy in the house the better, she said. I asked her why. She just said that some of the servants gossip. I hope that is all she meant. Annette is very discreet. She has been Mama's waiting woman ever since Mama was a girl. Mama sent her to fetch a bowl of water to bathe the wound. He has a fever in his leg. I stayed to help, but I was not much use – I do not like the sight of blood and had to keep turning my eyes away. When Mama cut away his breeches from the wound he bit his lip as if he was trying to stop himself from crying out. His face was white. I felt so sorry for him.

François stood guard outside the room to warn us of anyone's approach. When Mama went to fetch medicine I put one of my hands on top of the boy's and then, I blush to think of it now, I told him a story – my favourite child's story – to take his mind off the pain. I even said that I always ask Mama to read it to me when I am ill! I rinsed out his handkerchief for him and put it to dry over the back of the chair. I gave him mine. I laid it on the pillow next to him. He will see it when he wakes.

Papa is expected home tonight. I wonder what Mama will tell him.

Later

I have just been to see our fugitive. I crept along the passage to Mama's room, looking around carefully to make sure that no one saw me. I did not want to frighten him so I called out my name softly, but he was asleep, his dark hair rumpled on the pillow. Annette was sitting with him. A tray with food on it lay untouched next to the bed. I long to know how he came to be hiding here, and what he is running away from, but it will have to wait until he is better.

Meudon, 16 August 1792

I went to see our fugitive before breakfast but the door was locked. Mama let me in later. She whispered to me to be quiet. He has eaten a little food, but I could see that he had been crying. My handkerchief was screwed up in a damp ball on the pillow. He must feel very lonely and frightened.

Meudon, 18 August 1792

Our fugitive was sitting up when I went to see him today. He smiled at me. Mama says he is a little better. His handkerchief was dry. I gave it back to him, but he says I can keep it. So I told him he could keep mine. When I picked up his handkerchief I saw that initials were embroidered in one corner – A de B. I was bursting to know what they stood for, so I asked him – then felt embarrassed. But he did not mind. He told me they stood for Armand de Beauvantes, and that it was his name. Mama has told me how he got wounded.

He is very brave. He went to the aid of an unarmed Swiss guard who was fleeing one of the National Guards. Armand fought off the guard, so that the Swiss guard was able to escape, but was wounded in the leg.

"I could not run with that wound," he told Mama, "so I lay down and pretended to be dead. I lay as still as I could. I pulled a dead National Guard's jacket over myself so that if anyone did see that I was alive they would leave me alone." When I think how brave he was I have a lump in my throat. He is a hero.

Meudon, 19 August 1792

With everything that has happened, I had quite forgot the plight of the King and his family – even our own dear priest. We still have no news of our priest, but we learnt today that the King and his whole family are prisoners. Before the fighting began they were escorted for safety to the old royal riding school in the palace – that is where the Assembly sits – but now they have been put in prison, in the Temple. It is extraordinary to think that our King is in prison! I can hardly believe it. The King's sister and the Queen's friend, the princesse de Lamballe, have nobly offered to share the family's imprisonment.

21

That is very brave of them. I do not think I would show so much courage. Papa says no harm will come to any of them, and that they are being well treated, but it must be awful to be in that big dark gloomy place. Imagine. Once Louis XVI lived in splendour in the great palace of Versailles. Now he is a prisoner in the city. The Temple is in northeast Paris. I saw it once, when we were driving across Paris and the coachman took the wrong turning. Its great towers made me shiver.

François is furious that Papa has not resigned from the Assembly. He can barely look him in the face. He still believes that it was all a plot to topple the King from his throne and Papa must have known about it. I can't think how he can think such an awful thing. Papa was not even there! Not many of the deputies were. I suppose they were afraid for their own safety. And surely he can tell how upset Papa is – he is as shocked as he was the day a mob armed with pikes and pistols stormed the palace in June, stuck the red cap of liberty on the King's head and made him drink the nation's health. But François will not even listen to me. He always thinks he knows best.

I do not know what Mama has told Papa about Armand, but Papa kissed my head and said that I was a kind girl. The little lines between his eyes have got deeper though. Poor Papa, he walks about the house as if the burdens of the whole country rest on his shoulders. And now he has Armand to worry about too.

I was sitting sewing in a corner of the salon just now when I heard Mama beg Papa to leave the Assembly. It is not the first time she has asked him this. I put my sewing aside and listened. New elections are being held for the Assembly very soon. Papa always says that the country needs voices of reason to speak on its behalf – now more than ever. "That," I heard Mama say, "is what I am afraid of. You are too honest for them." Mama is right. Papa says what he thinks and it is dangerous to say what you think unless it is what the Jacobins want to hear (whoever they are). But Papa will make his own mind up. He is quite as stubborn as François – so Mama says!

Meudon, 20 August 1792

I am trying to write, lying on my bed. Wolf sits next to me, his rough head on my legs. I have sorely neglected him, these past few days, though I did take him to play with Armand. Armand confided to me that he likes dogs. He is able to hobble about now, but he has to do it very quietly so that no one will hear. He says his leg is stiff from lack of use.

I am so sad. Papa could not deliver my letter. Claire's family is not in Paris. Everyone who has not already left the city is leaving now. All my friends have gone. Armand will leave too soon. Armand is in the attic now. He was taken there, as soon as he could manage the stairs. I found a shoe buckle on the top stair, and took it up to him. I felt sure it was his. Few people wear shoe buckles now and it is a very fine one, though the clasp is slightly damaged. Papa gave all his shoe buckles away years ago – as did all the nobles who sat in the Assembly then. It is fortunate that I found it before any of the servants did, or they might have wondered whose it was and gone up to the attic to find out. He was very pleased that I had found it, and thanked me.

Mama is relieved to have her chamber to herself again, and in that wing Armand should not be disturbed. No one ever goes there.

Meudon, 22 August 1792

The Prussians have crossed the border and captured two of our fortresses. François spends most of his time now poring over Papa's maps and plotting their likely route to Paris. He has shown me where the fortresses are – at Longwy and Verdun. I'd like to know what Armand thinks about it all – the Revolution, the war and the King's imprisonment – but I feel too shy to ask. He must be a royalist, to have gone to the aid of a Swiss guard in the battle. What would Papa think of that? Papa may be an aristocrat by birth, but he is not a royalist! He was voted in as a deputy by the ordinary people.

François says it will not be long before the Prussian army enters Paris and that the Parisians will run away in terror. I think he is wrong. Has he not heard the cannon firing from the city? Even though it is hot I have to keep my windows closed to shut out the noise. Parisians are volunteering in huge numbers to fight the enemy. Marie says that there are thousands of men ready to defend the city and lay down their lives for their country.

But François is convinced that the French army is no match for the Prussians. They have lost many of their best officers, who are mostly aristocrats, since General Dillon was murdered earlier this year and those who are flocking to join up now are untrained volunteers who have never even held a musket before. Papa says that is true. But I wonder what it means for us. I mean, which side are we on? Has François even thought at all about that? Papa has always supported the Revolution. And he still sits in the Assembly that governs France. What would happen to him if the Prussians did march into Paris? I pray that he is not elected to the new Assembly.

Meudon, 23 August 1792

Papa went back to Paris today. All I know is that it is on business. I hope that business is nothing to do with the elections. He must be wracked with worry about how to get Armand away safely. I know I am. At least Armand's wound is healing nicely and is hidden by his breeches – an old pair of François's. So unless he is recognized no one will know he was in the battle. And I cannot imagine that in all the chaos anyone would recognize him. He is just a boy, who stepped in to save someone – not someone important like the Governor of the Tuileries who has gone into hiding. Even he has not been discovered yet, though Papa says he will be. It would be very hard for the Governor to escape without being recognized. But even so, I cannot help worrying. How will Armand get away? He has no papers and a passport is needed now if you wish to travel in France – even from one area to another.

François says that you can get hold of false papers if you know how and have enough money. François does seem to know the most extraordinary things, but I can't think how he knows about this.

Meudon, 24 August 1792

As I went to practise my harp just now I heard Marie say that the authorities are searching houses in the city. They're hunting for conspirators. All sorts of people are being accused of conspiracy and imprisoned.

When the farmer came by with eggs he said that he saw priests being pushed along the city streets yesterday. Is it any wonder that many of them did take the oath of loyalty. Those who have stood by their beliefs are very brave. I pray for our priest's safety every night. I cannot believe that all these people are plotting against the country. It is even being put about that the events of 10 August were a royal plot. It is said that conspirators lurk everywhere and that as soon as the volunteer soldiers depart for the front they will release the criminals in prison who will murder all good patriots. I felt frightened when I heard that – not because I believe such stories – but because it seems that just hiding someone could make you a conspirator. What would happen if the authorities decide to search *our* house. Papa is a good patriot, but will that protect us? Marie says they are also searching houses, demanding that all weapons are

27

handed over. There are not enough weapons to arm all the volunteers. So they might come here just for that.

Meudon, 25 August 1792

Armand left today. I am sorry, I will miss him, yet I am infinitely relieved that he has gone. I have not been able to sleep for worrying.

A friend of Papa's arrived in his carriage this morning to take Armand home. He was to travel as his nephew. We bundled him into the carriage as soon as it arrived. I pray that none of the servants saw him. I ran upstairs to watch as the carriage trundled off down the drive – a humble coach, it did not look as if it had ever belonged to an aristocrat, which I suppose is a good thing. Then I went up to the attic to make sure that he had left nothing behind – just in case the authorities do come to search the house. Annette was there tidying away the blankets and bolster. She smiled at me, and pulled something out of her pocket. "Monsieur le comte (Armand) told me to give you this, mademoiselle," she said in a whisper – as if it was a great secret. I took it eagerly wondering what it could be. I ran back to my chamber. It was a scrap of paper wrapped round a shoe buckle.

The note said: thank you for helping me. I will never forget and will always be at the service of you and your family. Then he signed his name. Armand. Underneath he had drawn his coat of arms. Only a royalist would do something like that. François would be pleased! When titles were abolished we had to remove our coat of arms from everything – even our carriages and our pew in church. I held the little buckle up to the light to see it sparkle. It was the buckle I'd found on the stair. And then, suddenly, looking at it, I felt as if I was back in the past, a little girl standing at the door, watching the ladies and gentlemen who used to fill our house, the balls, the dinners, the soirées, the musicians playing. Papa once said that better times for France lie ahead. Does he still believe that? Even now, when so many good and brave people are living in fear?

I will treasure that buckle always.

Meudon, 26 August 1792

I keep Armand's shoe buckle wrapped in his handkerchief, under the jewellery in my jewellery box. I took it out and looked at it several times this morning. It gives me a funny feeling. It will always remind me of him. I've kept the little note too. I'm glad I have them. Otherwise I might one day think it was all just a dream.

Meudon, 27 August 1792

Last night I dreamt that someone was hiding in the attic. The dream felt so real that I had to go up to the attic to make sure that I was wrong. I crept along the passage to the room where we'd hidden Armand. I was about to go in when I heard the floor creak behind the door. I felt the hair stand up on my arms. Someone *was* in there. For several minutes I stood, my hand on the doorknob, unsure whether to go in or not. The creak got louder – someone was coming towards the door. It swung open suddenly and François stood there, a spyglass in his hand. I was so relieved that it was only him that I burst out laughing. François looked at me as if I was mad.

Before he could ask why I was there I asked him what he was doing. He told me that he was looking for Prussian soldiers! I asked if I could have a look. He handed the spyglass to me and I held it up to my eye. Of course I couldn't see any, but to tease him I pretended that I could. "I can see a column marching up to the city gates," I said. "I recognize the uniform. They are Prussians." He believed me! I suppose because he was so desperate to. He grabbed the spyglass back, but of course he could see nothing. "Can you not see them?" I said. "Then they must have marched back to Prussia." François put the spyglass down and glared at me. He looked so annoyed that I ran away. I couldn't help laughing.

Meudon, 29 August 1792

I have just read what I wrote a few days ago, but I don't feel much like laughing now. I don't want to hide anyone, I don't want even to think about what is happening in France. I want everything to go back to how it was before this hateful Revolution began. Is it selfish of me to wish that? I truly do not wish anyone to suffer or go hungry, but I am tired of feeling frightened all the time. I wake up feeling afraid, and go to bed scared. Whenever the windows are open all I ever seem to hear is cannon booming. The news is always bad. I ask Marie to leave me a lit candle by my bed every night now. Oh, *when* will it end?

They are arresting all the wrong people – people who have done nothing wrong. Our neighbour's manservant Jean has just been to see us. He was in a terrible state. His master was taken away to Paris for questioning last night.

Jean swears that his master is innocent of any crime. He does not know who else to turn to. His master's family is far away. We did not even know his master was here. He has not been to call on us and we haven't seen his carriage for many weeks. Mama has sent a servant to Paris with a message for Papa to see what he can do. Papa has influential friends in the Assembly. Jean was so grateful that there were tears in his eyes. He wiped them away with his sleeve when he thought we weren't looking. I am proud of my parents and how they always try to help others. But I confess a part of me wishes he had asked someone else to help him. I want Papa to come home. I do not want him to stay in the city any longer than he must. It is not a safe place to be.

Meudon, 31 August 1792

Good news! Our neighbour – who had been put in prison – has been freed. I don't know where he is now, but I saw him when he came to thank Papa. Papa said that he was glad what little influence he still had had been put to some good use.

Meudon, 1 September 1792

François has been hunting for a place that we can ALL hide in! And this afternoon he came rushing up to me to say that he had found it. I tucked Wolfie under my arm and reluctantly followed him. Its entrance is in the sunken garden, under a slab in the centre. I crouched down to watch while François pulled away the slab to show me. He must have done this a few times because it came away very easily.

I held Wolf tightly so he wouldn't fall in, and peered in to the hole. It was cold and smelt musty and damp, like a cellar and it was so dark that I couldn't see how far down it went. I called softly into it and heard my voice echo against the walls. I couldn't imagine that anyone would want to hide in there. It would be like hiding in a dungeon. François wanted to climb down into it. I told him he was mad. Did he even know how far down it went? I demanded. What if he fell and hurt himself? How would he ever get out again?

"How like a girl," François muttered. "Always finding problems." He fetched a rope, knotted it in places to make footholds, and said that if I lowered it down, he could climb down and up again.

33

"But I'll never be able to pull you out," I pointed out. François is only a year older than me, but bigger and heavier. He looked quite taken aback. Of course he hadn't thought of that. How like a boy!

"Then I will lower you," he said suddenly. I shook my head vigorously. No, he would not.

He pushed the slab back into place crossly with his foot. I hope I've heard the end of that, but I feel sure I haven't.

I was right. Late this afternoon François came in search of me, a jubilant smile on his face. He had found what he believed to be another entrance to the hole, in the wine cellar. I was quite impressed.

"How did you know where to look?" I asked him. "The smell," he said.

"That hole smelt of wine. Did you not smell it too?" We went down to the wine cellar together. There is a door in the cellar wall, which I don't think can have been opened for years. It was very stiff. François used his hunting knife to scrape away the rust. He is stupid. It has got bent. Then he picked up his candle and beckoned to me to follow. I did though I did not like to. It was very cold. I propped open the door so that we could be sure of getting out again. François would not have thought of that.

When we reached the end of the passage François held the candle up to the roof. "That must be it," he said excitedly,

34

pointing upwards. I could see the slab. It was not many feet above our heads. "If one of us stands on the other's shoulders," François said, "we can get out that way."

I had no desire to crawl up a dirty tunnel, but I let him climb on to my shoulders, though I nearly buckled under his weight and had to hold on to the walls so that I didn't topple over. I gasped at him to hurry as he pushed up at the slab and then I felt his weight ease and he was out. He grinned back down at me. "I will meet you back in the cellar," he said. I was glad that I had the candle to light my way back. It was not far, but I raced along that passage as fast as I could. I didn't want to stay in that place any longer than I needed to.

It was only when I was back in my chamber that I saw my dress. The hem is dirty. And there are muddy boot prints on each shoulder. I am *not* pleased!

Meudon, 3 September 1792

François says he knows that something frightful is happening in Paris. I asked him how he knew. He said he has ears! So do I, but I am not sure I want to use them.

Meudon, 5 September 1792

I have learnt something that cheers me. Papa is not standing for the new Assembly. But he looks grave and unhappy and I wish I knew what was on his mind. Mama's face is almost as grave as Papa's. At supper he and Mama kept glancing at each other and their eyes plainly said, we must not speak of it in front of the children.

I think a noble would have to be very brave to stand for the new Assembly. Not many are. Even in the last Assembly, few nobles were appointed deputies, though the King's cousin, the duc d'Orléans is standing again – as a deputy for Paris. (All the regions in France have deputies to represent them.) He did not flee France, like the King's brothers. The Duke was very popular with the people. Papa says he has ambitions, though that is all he will say. What can they be? Surely he cannot expect to be made king now! He sits with the Jacobins in the Assembly. François says that the Jacobins hold very extreme views. It seems odd that the King's cousin chooses to sit with them. Does he think that will protect him?

Wolf has been banished to the kennels! He is in disgrace – and so am I. It is not fair. I did not chew up Papa's wig, but it is my fault Papa says for letting "that dog" run all over the house! Papa was looking for his wig and found it on the floor – a soggy mess. Wolf must have climbed on to the chair in the entrance hall where Papa had dropped it. Papa doesn't like wearing a wig and often tosses it there when he comes into the house. It made Wolf sick – there were little puddles all across the hall. Gaspard had to mop it up. I felt sorry for him but he gave me such a dirty look. It quite took me aback. He's never looked at me like that before.

I have been down to see Wolf in his new home, in the kennels near the stables where we used to keep the hunting dogs. He looked as miserable as I felt. Mama says that in a day or so Papa will have forgotten and Wolf can come back inside. But should it ever happen again … and she looked at me sternly. It is not my fault!

I wish I could forget how Gaspard looked at me.

Meudon, 6 September 1792

Our house was searched last night! The guards said they had only come for arms for the volunteers but they had a good look around many of the rooms too. I felt sure they wanted to see that we hadn't got any *person* hidden as well. What would we have done if Armand had still been hidden in our attic? If only Wolf was bigger – he could have barked and warned us.

They made such a noise when they came – battering on the door with their pikes. I was terrified. But I knew I'd feel safer up than in my room on my own, so I pulled my shawl round my shoulders and tiptoed down the landing. François had woken too, and crept along to join me. We crouched there together. He put an arm round my shoulders – to protect me, he said. But I could feel from how tightly he squeezed that he was just as scared as me.

I sat as still as I could, and peeped down. The hall was full of men in uniform. I counted about a dozen of them. Papa looked and sounded quite composed as if there was nothing frightening about armed men battering on the door at night. Pierre was sent to fetch Grandpapa's old musket. If I hadn't been so scared I'd have laughed. It's ancient and if you fire it you're as likely to take off your own head as the enemy's. No one has dared use it for years and it's all cobwebby and dusty. The officer in charge took it gingerly from Pierre. They must be desperate to take something like that. François did not tell them about his sword. He'd die rather than surrender that.

They didn't go into the cellar. We had pushed a rack of wine bottles over in front of the entrance to hide it, though you'd never suspect there was a passage behind it. It comforts me now to think there is somewhere in the house we can hide if we need to, but it comforts me not at all to think that we might.

I will ask Mama if Wolf may come back into the house.

Meudon, 7 September 1792

I am trying to write, Wolf curled up on my knee. I push him off but he just clambers up again. I am not sure that he will ever grow big and brave. He is so soft, more like a kitten than a puppy. I was so miserable without him. As soon as Mama gave me permission, I ran to the kennels to unchain him. He was so excited to see me. He ran round and round my ankles, and jumped up and down all the way back to the house. He will sleep on my bed again tonight. But I have warned him to leave Papa's slippers alone. Papa will keep leaving them out and Wolf is very interested in them.

Meudon, 22 September 1792

A republic has been declared in France. The servants have been chattering about it all day. They do not speak of it in front of me, but I caught what they were saying. When they thought I wasn't looking I saw them giving me sympathetic looks, as if I am to be pitied, which makes me feel peculiar. Gaspard is delighted. I heard him singing in the pantry as he polished the silver. He gave me a triumphant look, as if he had won – and we had lost. I don't know if that makes sense, but I cannot think how else to describe it. He makes me feel quite uneasy. Up until now I have always taken our servants' loyalty for granted. Gaspard has not been with us as long as some of the others, but until the day he had to clear up Wolf's mess I had not thought that he might actually dislike us.

Meudon, 24 September 1792

Papa has tried to explain to us about the Republic. Two days ago the new France was born. I think that's what he means. It is called Year One of French Liberty, One and Indivisible. What a mouthful. I'll never be able to remember all that. I feel as if they – those Jacobins – are trying to sweep away everything that reminds people of the old regime. What does this mean for the King? And for us? We aristocrats are as much a part of that past. Are we to be swept away with it?

Meudon, 10 October 1792

My uncle and his family are coming to stay, on their way to Rouen. They will not be staying with us for long. Rouen is supposed to be a safe place, I suppose that means safe for royalists. Uncle is a royalist, or at least his views on the Revolution are quite different to Papa's. I've often heard them argue about it. I wish they could stay for longer. I am sad because it is a long time since I saw them and I think it will be a very long time before we see them again. My cousin Lucie is the same age as me. It will be so nice to have a *girl* to talk to.

Meudon, 15 October 1792

I am desolate. I cannot bear to even look at Papa, which makes me feel quite dreadful. I have learnt why my relations left their home. The princesse de Lamballe has been murdered. She was just one of those in the prisons who were killed. An awful lot of prisoners have been murdered, many of them priests. I heard my uncle talk about it to Papa and Mama. What seems to have happened is this. The Princess was taken from the Temple to another prison, where she was asked to swear an oath of loyalty to the nation, and another of hatred of the King and Queen. She agreed to the former, but refused the latter. For that she was battered to death, her head cut off and stuck on a pike, which was waved under the window of the Temple prison for the Queen to see. How hateful! I have been talking to François about it. In his opinion the murders were planned by some of the members of the Assembly. Their names he says are Robespierre, Danton and Marat.

And it is they, and their friends in the Paris Commune – that he says is the name of the authority that now runs the city – who are now the real rulers of the country. I felt my blood run cold. The murders took place before the new Assembly sat. Papa was a member of that Assembly. I can scarcely bear to write what I am going to write now. How can Papa not have known what was happening? Could he not have done *anything* to stop it? It is terrible to me to think that he sat by and did nothing.

It is said that the people in the prisons were killed for conspiring with France's enemies. They were murdered to make us safe! How could anyone believe such a thing! The killings were carried out by people called "sans-culottes". Most of them arrived in Paris from Marseille in July, but many of them aren't even French. François says that they were given the name "sans-culottes" because they wear trousers not breeches, as some workmen do.

It must be because of the massacres that we have seen so many carriages driving out of Paris these past weeks. Anyone who can is fleeing the capital. I feel sorrier and sorrier for the royal family. What will be their fate?

Meudon, 17 October 1792

My cousins left today. Lucie confided to me that she was dreading the journey. She said that their carriage had often been stopped on the way here for their papers to be checked, but at least it is not far from here to Rouen. We have promised to write to each other often. I wish I was going with them. I wish I could take Wolf and never come back. I'd miss François though, and Mama.

Meudon, 18 October 1792

Awoke drenched in sweat. The Princess's death haunts me. I have nightmares about it nearly every night. But tonight in my dream it was not the Princess's head I saw waved on a pike. I pulled Wolf close to me. He snuggled up in the crook of my arm. It comforts me to wake and feel that he is there. I cannot bear to be alone at night now.

Meudon, 19 October 1792

I have been barely able to look at Papa since learning about the massacres, and he must have noticed because today he asked what ailed me. I quite forgot myself and it all burst out of me – all the disgust I'd been feeling. I told him about my nightmares, I told him I could not understand how such terrible things could happen. I did not accuse him in words, but the truth of how I felt must have been clear in my eyes. He said he had hoped to keep the news of it from me. He said he was sorry I had learnt about it, and that he was as upset as I was. The Princess was a good woman, who did not deserve her fate. He must have seen that I still did not believe him, because he patted the seat next to him, told me to sit down, then talked to me as if I was truly grown up. He explained how real power had been taken away from the Assembly by the Paris Commune. The Commune had been granted the power to arrest people suspected of trying to bring down the Revolution and there are many such people, he insisted. He reminded me that we were at war too. Special powers are granted to those in charge at times like these. But he never believed that such terrible deeds would be committed. I find it hard to understand what is going on. To me the Revolution seems to have gone all wrong, and I said so. Papa nodded gravely, as if he understood how I felt. Then I suddenly remembered how he had helped Armand escape, and had helped to free our neighbour and I felt ashamed to have thought that Papa would ever do a bad thing. I put my arms around him to show that I was sorry and he put his round me, and we sat together quietly for a long time.

Meudon, 30 October 1792

The war is going well for the Republic. Our armies seem to be winning on all fronts now – but they are invading other lands too. Nice and Savoy are now part of France. I do not think that is right. A great victory has been won at a place called Jemappes – and General Dumouriez has led his victorious army into Brussels and planted a Tree of Liberty there. Émigrés who fled to Belgium will now have to find somewhere else to live. François once said that the French were no match for the Austrians and Prussians. But these victories have quite put the lie to that. François is not always right even if he thinks he is.

Meudon, 19 November 1792

We have learnt that the French army is not invading other countries, it is "liberating" them – from tyrants and oppressors like our King. Our government will help any people that seek to be free. I don't think I'd welcome in an invading army, even if I were one of the oppressed. But our armies are greeted with much joy, we are told. Humph. How can anyone welcome in an army whose government locks up its King and Queen and murders hundreds of innocent people?

It is over three months now since the royal family was imprisoned in the Temple. How they are faring, we know not. I often think of them.

Meudon, 28 November 1792

Papa has just returned from Paris. He brought me back a print of the Battle of Jemappes. They are being sold on every street corner in the city. There is even a play put on about it

47

and it is so popular with the Parisians that you cannot get a seat to see it. The company performing it used to perform before the Queen. I know actors must earn their living but that feels like a betrayal to me. I hope the Queen never learns of it. I have learnt something else too. The deputies are meeting to decide the King's fate.

Meudon, 30 November 1792

This morning a courier rode up with letters. I was thrilled to find there was one for me. I opened it eagerly. It was from my cousin Lucie. They arrived at Rouen without mishap. She asks for news, but has little news to tell me. She begs to know when we will visit them. I cannot think when that will be. Sometimes I think we will be here for ever.

I have resolved to write anything important in invisible ink. François has showed me how to do this. It is a messy business though and I had to tear up my first letter to Lucie because I got sticky bits of lemon on the paper. You fill your quill with the clear juice of a fruit like lemon or orange and then write across the page – exactly as if you were writing with ink. No one can see what you have written unless you hold the page to the heat of a candle.

I have written that she will need to read the letter *properly* by candlelight – I underlined that part. I hope she will understand what I mean.

So – here is what I wrote to Lucie. THE KING IS TO BE PUT ON TRIAL! I am astonished that such important news has not reached them. I wrote this in invisible ink at the end of the letter, in case the letter should fall into the wrong hands. Who knows how many hands letters pass through now? Or whose eyes scan them, or who breaks open the seal? François says that I should write *everything* in invisible ink now. And Papa has cautioned us to be careful who we write to.

So, the King's trial. I learnt about it when an English friend of Papa's called by on his way to Calais. (I hid behind a curtain.) His judges are to be the elected deputies. I am thankful that Papa is not a deputy now so will not be called on to vote on the King's fate.

"They condemn themselves if they find him innocent. They condemn themselves if they find him guilty," Papa's friend said. I don't know what crime the King is accused of but I feel sure he will be found guilty of something. If not, they would have to put him back on the throne – so the English friend thinks. They will never do that! What will his fate be if he is found guilty? In England they chopped off a king's head. François says they would not dare do so here. That would bring down the wrath of all Europe on us and we

are at war with half of it already. So he will stay in prison –
unless someone manages to break in and free him. And he
will be too well guarded for that.

Meudon, 3 December 1792

I had a fright this morning. One of the maids turned the
mattress, gave it a good thumping and out fell my diary! I
nearly had a fit! I kicked it away under the bed before she
saw it. But what if I hadn't seen it first? What if someone
had picked it up and read it? I must find a better hiding
place for it.

Mama is more fortunate than me. She has the perfect
hiding place for her writings – a little writing desk, which has
a lock and key, so they are quite safe from prying eyes.

Meudon, 11 December 1792

The King was called to the National Convention today (that
is the name of the new Assembly) to hear his indictment

and face his accusers for the first time. Gaspard crows that "Louis Capet" will soon be called upon to hold the hot hand. I asked Marie what he meant. Her eyes flashed indignantly. How dare that man talk about our anointed King in such a way, she said. I hope she doesn't speak so freely in front of Gaspard, or she could find herself hauled up before the authorities as a royalist spy.

I still don't understand what Gaspard meant. Marie won't say though I am sure she knows. What *is* the hot hand?

Meudon, 25 December 1792

Christmas is nearly over. We none of us felt like celebrating and left the servants to make merry. The King is to return to the Convention for his trial tomorrow. He has been kept apart from his family since he first appeared at the Convention on the 11th of this month, but has sometimes been permitted to see them. A bitter Christmas it must be for them.

Documents have been found locked in an iron box at the palace which, it is claimed, prove the King's guilt beyond question. I still don't know what he has been accused of. But what will the verdict be?

Gaspard has asked permission to attend the trial.

51

Spectators are admitted to the public gallery. Papa has granted permission. He would not dare do otherwise.

Meudon, 4 January 1793

Today the deputies will vote on whether they find the King innocent or guilty. If they find him guilty they will vote again to decide his sentence. There might be an appeal to the people.

Meudon, 10 January 1793

My uncle writes from Rouen that there has been rioting in the town. The King's trial has upset many people and sympathy for him is increasing.

Meudon, 15 January 1793

The King has been found guilty by a majority of the deputies. There is to be no appeal to the people. That is just what I expected.

Meudon, 16 January 1793

Today the deputies deliver their verdict – they will have to stand up in front of *everyone*, and give it, one by one. The *death sentence* hangs over the King's head. How can it have come to this? But will any of the deputies be brave enough to acquit him? It would take much courage. The gallery will be crammed with spectators, who are sure to make their feelings plain – and I doubt the King will find any supporters amongst them, at least none that will admit to it.

I am mightily relieved that Papa is no longer a deputy. What an ordeal it will be.

Meudon, 17 January 1793

A majority of the deputies have voted for death. In my wildest dreams I did not think it would come to this. To Papa the decision has not come as a surprise. When Marie brought me the news I fell into her arms and wept. François stormed out of the room, and even out of the house. He took so long to return that I was afraid that he had ridden away, but he has returned now.

Even the King's cousin – the duc d'Orléans, who is now known as Philippe-Egalité – voted for death. He was the last of the Paris deputies to speak. What will the King say when he learns of his cousin's vote? François has nothing but scorn for him. But would François have been brave enough to stand up and acquit the King? Who would wish to be a Bourbon in these dark days?

We are praying for a reprieve.

Meudon, 20 January 1793

There is to be no reprieve. The execution will take place in the morning. The King will be allowed to see his family. I cannot write more for weeping.

Meudon, 21 January 1793

The King was executed this morning. Up until the very moment it happened I clung to the hope that it would not, that the people would rebel against such a sentence.

I could not sleep. At first light I was at the window. Bitterly cold though it was, I flung it wide and stared out towards the city. I could see nothing. Paris was shrouded in fog. I could not stop shivering and Marie wrapped a shawl around my shoulders. She urged me to dress. I shook my head. I could not take my eyes away from the city. The fog was beginning to lift. I could just see the tops of towers, the spires of churches. But I still couldn't hear anything.

François put his spyglass in my hands. We took turns to peer through it.

Muffled drumbeats rolled across the valley towards us.

I felt rather than saw the closed carriage clatter along the silent streets of the city, bearing the King on his last journey on earth. The carriage stops. The King descends, and climbs the few steps to the scaffold.

What does he see as he looks about himself for the last time? Outside my window a rook caws. François's fingers tighten on my shoulders. The drums stop rolling. An awful silence falls. I am aware that Mama and Papa have come to stand behind me. No one speaks. It is a solemn moment – the execution of a king.

A single cannon booms across the valley. It is done. A thousand cheers drift from the city towards us.

Meudon, 7 February 1793

I have not kept up my diary. After the recent awful event, I have felt too dispirited to write. François is still sunk in gloom. He broods constantly about the King's fate. There is a rumour that some young nobles planned to rescue him, and François despises himself for not joining them.

It is well he did not. I wish he would stop moping. I am trying to keep busy. I am embroidering a handkerchief for Mama. This task is not much to my liking, but I know it will give her pleasure. I practise my harp diligently – a full half hour every day! M Le Blanc would be pleased, but it is many months since we have seen him. Mama has not played the pianoforte since the King's execution, but this evening she sat down at it again. Wolf lay on my lap, Papa was lying back in his chair, eyes closed but with a smile on his face as she played, as if his mind was filled with pleasant memories.

For a little while I forgot about the Revolution. I felt almost as I did before it began. I am trying not to dwell on the past. It only makes me miserable. We must look to the future, Papa says.

Meudon, 8 February 1793

France has declared war on Great Britain and the Dutch Republic. Is there any country in Europe that we are not at war with? François has roused himself but he spends most of his time in the library poring over his precious maps. He is trying to follow the progress of the allies' (enemy) forces, but it is not easy. We are not always sure where they are! Even though we are so near Paris it is not always possible to get news.

Meudon, 10 February 1793

I am writing near the window where the light is best. Outside Pierre is chopping wood. It is bitterly cold. He stops and stamps his feet then clasps his arms around himself for warmth. It is Gaspard's job, but Gaspard has gone to a meeting of Jacobins at the local club. I must say, he spends an awful lot of time at meetings. There is ice on the inside of my chamber window. I have a fire in my room, but it is a poor little fire that does not give out much heat and I have to sit very close to it to keep warm. I wish Mama would allow it to be built up more, but she says we must use the wood sparingly. But though we have less than we had, we are fortunate. Many do not have the means of enduring the cold. Mama has arranged for fuel to be sent to the poor in the neighbourhood.

I can see Paris through the bare arms of the tree outside my window. My city. I used to love it, but now I wish it was further away. The towers glower like teeth in a wicked jaw.

Marie says there has been more trouble in the city. She does not say what, and I do not ask.

Wolf has been scratching at my door and I have got up to let him in. He has a most guilty expression on his face so I hope he has not been up to mischief. He has jumped up on to the bed, right on to my diary. And now I have big paw prints all over the page I have just written. Naughty Wolf!

Meudon, 15 March 1793

Today we were visited by a delegation from the authorities. They have a new committee whose job it is to spy on everyone. They want to know everything, even how much flour you have in your kitchen (one small bag, enough for one loaf). They are making sure that we aren't hoarding anything that should go to the city or to the brave volunteers fighting at the front. After they'd finished in the kitchen, they had a good look round the cellar. I suppose we are lucky they didn't empty it. Some of the men were surly and disrespectful. What upset us most is that two of them are known to us. Mama sent money to their sons when they volunteered for the war. They are poor, so it meant they'd have food and boots, unlike many who have volunteered.

I was relieved when they tramped away at last.

Can they not understand what a good patriot Papa is and leave us alone? François says he expected that this would happen. It does not matter that Papa was a deputy, he says, they will never forget that we are aristocrats. But we are *not* aristocrats now. We are citizens of France like everyone else.

Meudon, 18 March 1793

Papa's steward, M Brouquart, has been to see him three times this week. I cannot imagine what business can be so urgent as to bring him here so often, nor have I been able to find out. I walk past the study door as often as I dare, but they keep their voices low. M Brouquart looks anxious, but always has a pleasant smile for me.

I wish I could say the same about our other servants. Gaspard seems to be watching us all the time. He creeps about everywhere. Marie says he has the forked tongue of a viper. She does not trust him any more than I do. He is clever though, he has said nothing that I can complain about. He whistles constantly that terrible revolutionary song called "Ça Ira". The words are all about how they will string up the aristocrats.

François and I hum it too – whenever we see Gaspard – just to show that we do not care.

I feel sorry for Pierre, who has to shoulder the extra work when Gaspard goes off to his meetings. He boasts that he is meeting important Jacobins. Pierre would be stupid to complain though. He may be diligent and hardworking but all that seems to matter now is where your loyalty lies. Gaspard's is to the Republic, Pierre's is to us. That is enough now to get Pierre into trouble.

Meudon, 20 March 1793

I cannot think how I would manage without my diary. But I know it is more important than ever now that I keep it safely hidden. I move it from place to place. I feel sick to think what might happen if the wrong person found it.

We were searched again today. The patrol came in the evening, when we were having supper. I am sure that is why they came then, to spoil our meal. Papa was as courteous as ever and even offered them food and wine. They accepted the wine, and Gaspard was made to fetch it. He did not look pleased, and cast us sour looks. The patrol came from Versailles. I can't think why. But I was not sorry not to see those rude guards again. This patrol made a very thorough search. They must have gone through ALL of Papa's books. It was a good thing for them that there were so many of them, or they'd have been here until dawn. Papa has a large library. Our meal was ruined by the time we were able to sit down and finish it, but Papa and Mama were far too polite and "gentil" to say anything. Not that I felt like eating after they had gone. None of us did.

They picked up every book and shook it. All that flew out of most of them was a lot of dust. What did they expect to find? Secret letters? And it was then that I realized just how careful I had to be. I go hot and cold thinking what would happen to us if anyone found my diary. All my secrets and private thoughts are written in this book, everything I think and feel – well, nearly everything. But certainly it would be enough to get us into a lot of trouble. But at least I am not as stupid or careless as my brother. (I will explain about that later.)

They did not find anything in the library. Ha! But then they went through all Papa's papers. Mama looked pale but Papa was perfectly calm as if it was the most normal thing in the world to read someone else's private papers. They didn't find anything. Papa is no traitor. Then it was Mama's turn. She was asked where she kept her private letters – "from your relations and friends". She brought them her little writing desk. They made her open it. So she had to fetch the key. Apart from some sheets of plain paper it was empty. Mama always burns her letters now. They did look disappointed. All this searching and they had found nothing! The officer was about to hand it back to Mama when a dry voice suddenly said: "I know these desks. They often have a secret drawer." I looked at the speaker. He was a short man with greasy skin and lank dark hair that looked as if he never washed it. I hadn't taken much notice of him up till then, but he must have been quite important for the others deferred to him. He took the desk from Mama and examined it very carefully. His pudgy fingers found the secret drawer easily and clicked it open. A smirk spread over his oily face but it vanished when he saw that it too was empty. He demanded if there was anything else — as if we had all sorts of incriminating letters hidden about the house. He made me feel like a criminal.

Someone brought him a map. They looked at each other and smiled. Aha, at last we have found something. It was a map of England. Why, Papa was asked accusingly, did he have a map of an enemy country in his possession? Papa said, perfectly reasonably, that if they looked closely at it they would see that it was an old one. It had belonged to his father. But, oily face said, jabbing a fat finger at a blob of ink where London was marked. "What is that?" Papa said it looked to him very much as if someone had spilt ink on the map. But the oily one was not satisfied. He rolled it up curtly

63

and handed it to an underling, who took it from him as carefully as if the secrets of a plot to overthrow the Republic were concealed in it. They took away a few papers, too, but I heard Papa say to Mama that they were not important and would do little other than send the poor man whose job it was to read such stuff to sleep. I pray so.

It is fortunate that they did not search François's room. He had something in there, which would have excited them far more than that old map. A map of France with each of the battles our ENEMIES have won marked on it in ink. He's even drawn a pair of crossed swords over the nearest towns. I begged him to burn it at once. What would we do if they came back and found it. I told him he was stupid.

"I didn't think," he said.

"That is just it," I said, "You don't think." He gave me such a hurt look.

Meudon, 10 April 1793

News reached us today that General Dumouriez has defected to the Austrians. Having failed to persuade the army to march on Paris, he and a few senior officers, which included the duc d'Orléans' son, the duc de Chartres, rode across to enemy lines. Papa says that they are traitors. François says this will be bad for the Duke – and for us.

Meudon, 15 April 1793

This will be the last entry I will write at Meudon for some time. Tomorrow we are going to our château in Picardy. Earlier today M Brouquart brought the papers we need. We are to travel under false names. The name on my passport is Hélène Dubois, and I am travelling as Mama and Papa's niece. François is travelling as a manservant and will have to sit on the box! It serves him right. He will have to do as he is told. How fortunate it is that our papers did not arrive until after our last house search! Papa and Mama are calm about our going. They do not want to alarm us, but I think I understand why we are leaving. Since the General's defection nobles are being closely watched. A special tribunal, the Revolutionary Tribunal, has been set up in Paris by order of the new Committee of Public Safety to try anyone *they* are suspicious of. François says the members of this committee are the true rulers of France now.

I am sad to leave, but at least I will no longer have to see Gaspard's surly face, as he creeps about the place, spying on us.

I thought that I would have to leave Wolf behind. It would have quite broken my heart. Papa said he would be too much trouble – I think he was wondering how we'd manage him on the journey – but I promised to take great care of him. In the end Papa said he could not resist my entreaties. I flung my arms around his neck and he said how happy it made him to see me smile again.

But I wish we were going anywhere but that gloomy place. Papa likes it, it reminds him of his childhood but it is chilly and dark. Most of all, I dread the journey. I am trying to pretend that it will be an adventure. I always thought that I would love to have an adventure but it's the sort of adventure this might be that bothers me.

We have not told anyone our true destination, simply that we are visiting friends. Papa says that the fewer people who know where we are going the better it will be for all of us.

Our boxes are packed. Marie packed for me, though she did not do it very well. She wanted to put in my finest gowns that I am sure I will never wear. I told her to take them out again. "I will not need them," I said.

"But mademoiselle, think of your *toilette*," she exclaimed aghast. I do not care about my *toilette* as much as Marie would like. But I allowed her to pack the blue dress she says I look best in. And in went the curling tongs, and the tortoiseshell hairbrush to dress my hair. She looked askance at the gown in which I am to travel. It is my oldest one, and she thinks it is quite unsuitable for a marquis's daughter, but I think it is perfect. And I am plain Hélène Dubois now.

I put together a few of my most precious things. The bracelet that belonged to Papa's mama, my pearl necklace, an antique brooch, and – Armand's shoe buckle. I sat and looked at it for a while. Then I wrapped it up in the handkerchief and put it with the rest of my things. Now, I am ready. So I will put away my diary and try to sleep. Tomorrow morning, early, we leave Meudon.

Château de Vaillegard, 16 April 1793

We have arrived. The château is quite as horrible as I remembered, but I was so relieved to get here at last. I am very tired. The journey took almost twice as long as we had expected.

We were welcomed by Gregoire, the caretaker, and his wife, the only servants who still live here. He is quite an old man, at least forty, but kindly. His wife I am less sure of, but she is polite and respectful.

Sitting here listening to the drip of water into the bucket – it has begun to rain and the roof leaks into my bedroom – I am trying not to think about our journey here. It took an age for, as well as all the stops to have our papers checked, the roads are very bad – I don't think they have been repaired at all since the Revolution began. The first time the coachman pulled up I felt very frightened, knowing that we were all travelling on false papers. And some of the guards asked so many questions. The National Guards are local people. One of them looked at us so attentively that I felt sure that he had recognized us. But he said nothing. Each time we stopped I expected to be told to descend and taken to the local police post. Papa's answer was always the same. He was a merchant, travelling with his wife and niece to visit friends in Picardy. Poor Papa. He hates lies.

Even the main roads were bad, huge potholes that we had to drive round, and how our ancient coach did squeak and rattle and swing about from side to side. But I dreaded the back roads and the routes that took us through forests more – they are much plagued by bandits and highwaymen. Worst of all was driving through towns. Our coach was stared at by the inhabitants and we had to drive slowly. We avoided them as much as we could.

I was mightily glad to be inside the coach, Wolf snuggled up on my lap, rather than perched outside like the poor coachman and François.

If it had not been for Wolf we might not have got here at all. Halfway through one of the small towns that we had no choice but to cross, we were stopped by a veritable giant of a man, who was smoking a pipe. He wore the red bonnet and trousers of a sans-culotte. We had already shown our papers to the guards and had received permission to continue but almost as soon as we moved off this man strode up to our carriage and bellowed at the coachman to stop. He gave no reason, but our poor coachman had to obey. I tried not to shrink back as he thrust his face right up to the window. His eyes scoured our faces. Suddenly he banged on the door and shouted: "Out". We looked at each other in consternation. Who was he? What did he want? Why must we descend? My heart began to beat hard. My worst fears were about to be realized. We were to be dragged away by this terrible man. Wolf was on my lap. In my terror I squeezed him too tightly and he yelped and struggled to get out of my arms. The man looked astonished to see a little dog crawl over the seat towards him, but to my surprise a slow smile spread over his face. "Ah, the petit chien. I have a little dog just like you," he said. Wolf wagged his tail. He is everyone's friend, unless they threaten me. I decided to take advantage of the sans-culotte's change of mood and leant forward.

"That is my name for him. How clever of you to know." The sans-culotte grinned broadly and indicated to me to open the door. I was terrified he would seize Wolf and bear him away and I would never see my poor little dog again, but I did not dare refuse. My fingers trembling I opened the door. The man reached in with one bare arm, picked up Wolf and stroked him. Wolf did not seem to mind. He even licked the man's face! (I told him he was disloyal later!) The man merely laughed, and thrust him back into the carriage. Then, to our huge relief, he shut the door and thumped it. "*Allez!*" The coachman didn't hesitate. He cracked his whip and we rolled away before he could change his mind.

As we drove through the square I saw that a pole had been erected there. Tricolour ribbons – red, white and blue, the colours of the Revolution – hung limply down its sides. Papa explained that it was a Tree of Liberty. They are being planted everywhere to celebrate the country's freedom from the tyranny of the old regime. Liberty, I thought, as I stared at it. It felt like a bad joke. I cannot remember what it is like to feel free.

I was stiff and sore by the time we reached the château. Jeanne, the caretaker's wife, had made us some broth, which we had with black bread – the only sort they can get now, she said gruffly. But we were so grateful that we devoured it eagerly. I had not eaten anything since early morning. I had felt too scared to be hungry but the smell of the hot broth made me realize how famished I was. Gregoire fetched some scraps for Wolf to eat. Jeanne did not look at all pleased. One more mouth to feed. I don't think Wolf likes her. But at least he didn't growl at her.

Château de Vaillegard, 18 April 1793

I am writing this in my new chamber. (I was given a new one after I told Mama that the other one leaked.) It is a smaller room, with a sloping ceiling, on the same floor. There is just room enough for the bed and a table and chair. The main sleeping apartments are on the floor below. But we are keeping to one wing on the floor above.

There is a crucifix over my bed. On the wall opposite hung a picture of the crucifixion. It is horrible and I have taken it down. Though the room is small, the window looks out on to the garden at the back, and beyond the garden fields stretch away as far as I can see.

Mama would like us to keep to the upper floors as much as possible. It has begun to dawn on me that no one except the caretaker and his wife knows that we are here, and that Mama and Papa would like to keep it that way.

We eat our meals in a room at the end of the wing. Gregoire's wife Jeanne brings them up. I was dismayed to see the small size of our portions. Jeanne has warned us that there will not be a lot to eat. Then I think she must be keeping food back from us for the countryside around here

71

is abundant and there is a vegetable garden, as well as farms on the estate. I can see the vegetable garden from my little window. Gregoire is digging in it now. I will ask Mama if I may go down to see it. I will take Wolf with me. He is in sore need of a walk.

Château de Vaillegard, 20 April 1793

Jeanne is not keeping back food from us. There are food shortages in France. Much of the farmers' produce has to be sold in the towns or sent to the soldiers at the front. I am ashamed of myself for harbouring such suspicions. They are good people.

If we are still here in the summer (and I hope fervently that we are not) there will be a feast of vegetables. Some of them at least must find their way to our table. Gregoire is proud of his garden. He has told me what he grows in it. If only I could go outside to see it, but Mama will still not let us go out. Jeanne said he should plant potatoes, but he refuses to.

"Potatoes. They are food fit only for pigs," he declares. I told him that the English eat potatoes. He snorted as if to say that is what he'd expect of those English savages. But I would dearly like to try one.

He is ashamed of the poor state of the gardens. But how can one man tend such a huge garden? It is much overgrown, weeds sprout between the stones of the paths and the fountains are broken. Papa is saddened to see it, he remembers when it looked very different, but at least it does not look as if a noble family is in residence here, which makes me feel safer.

Château de Vaillegard, 21 April 1793

François and I have been exploring the château. Mama and Papa have relaxed a little. We still live in our upper rooms but so long as we are careful we are allowed to go downstairs, in the day. At night, we keep to our upstairs rooms. We cannot even have a light – Mama is afraid that someone will see it – so we go early to bed.

Now I will describe the château. It is really more like a castle than a country house. There are turrets and battlements – and François says that there is even a dungeon. He found it when he was exploring the cellars and vaults, where the wine is stored. I am glad I do not have to go down there to fetch it. I thought that he had just found another cellar until he told me that there were iron chains fixed into the wall and that damp drips from the ceiling. I don't like to think that I am living on top of a dungeon. I have not forgotten how I hated going into that dark passage in our house in Meudon. François says the château is haunted. He told me that the ghost of a murdered ancestor stalks the battlements outside our windows, his bloodied head under his arm. I put my hands over my ears and told him to stop – he was frightening me. He has been reading about our family's history in the library, and swears it is true.

I am writing in the dark, my bed sheet draped over me. The moon is full but I daren't go near the window in case That Thing is still prowling the terrace outside. Wolf is of little comfort. He is hiding under the bed. Oh, if only I could have a candle. François was right! The château *is* haunted. I was woken by a noise that sounded as if something or someone was outside the window, but I was far too scared to go and see. I slid down to the bottom of my bed and pulled the sheet right up over my head. I lay there as still as I could and tried not to think about the ghost. But it was hard not to. Every time a floorboard creaked I shivered. Every floorboard in this place creaks when the wind blows and it is howling tonight. It whistles through every crack and keyhole. I dread to think what it will be like here in winter.

Château de Vaillegard, 5 May 1793

When I was exploring the château this morning I found a fortepiano in a corner of the salon! (It isn't easy to see downstairs, the rooms are all in shadow even in bright sunshine, the shutters are kept closed and there are dustcovers over all the furniture.) I asked Mama to play to us, but she will not. She says she has not played the fortepiano since she was a girl and that she has no music. I was surprised. I thought she would have brought some with her. Mama loves her music, and here she can play all day if she chooses. I am determined to find her something to play. If there is a fortepiano here there must be music too.

I searched all over the library for music and my search has been rewarded! Kind Gregoire brought me a pair of library steps – even those were covered up – so that I could reach up to the top shelves and I am glad he did for it was on the very top shelf that I found some music – Bach and Handel sonatas and some Italian airs.

I showed Mama what I had found. I thought she would be pleased. I thought she would sit down at the fortepiano at once. But she has not. After all my efforts too. I am most disappointed. I cannot think why she will not play to us. No one but us will hear her.

Château de Vaillegard, 1 June 1793

I am ashamed to say that I have not been keeping up my diary. In truth, I can't really be bothered. I have all the time I need to write now but so little to write about. I wish I was allowed to go outside more often, but the farmer comes up to the château frequently and Mama is afraid that he will see us. I have seen him from the window. He looked up once when I was looking out, and I crouched down quickly. He has a cheery face and I feel sure he would not betray us even if he did see us. And he is one fresh face to look upon. I am sick of seeing no one but us, Gregoire and Jeanne.

Is this what it feels like to be a prisoner?

Poor Wolf. He feels like a prisoner too. I walk him up and down the courtyard but he yearns for a proper walk. I am sorry, I tell him. But it is not my fault. At least I don't have to worry about his food. Gregoire always manages to find him scraps to eat. I am grateful to him for that. He even offered to walk him. I accepted his offer gladly, but though Wolf trotted off happily enough, he sat down and refused to move when he saw that I was not coming too.

I haven't been down to the garden once this week, but from my window I can see green leaves springing up in the vegetable plot. It is very neatly tended – Gregoire loves his vegetables – so soon we should have more to eat. I hope so! I am always hungry. When I look at myself in the looking glass I am sure that my face has grown thinner. My gowns hang more loosely on me too. If I get any thinner Mama will have to take them in.

The sun is blazing now, and even when the window is open my little room gets unbearably hot. It is so quiet and I am dreadfully bored.

Château de Vaillegard, 5 June 1793

Gregoire brought us our meal today and I heard him whisper to Papa that there is strife in Paris. I was all ears! I heard nothing more but he left a newspaper behind and when no one was about I took it away to read. I could not make much sense of it, but from what I can understand it seems that there has been a struggle for power in the Convention between the Jacobins, who are the radical group and the more moderate group, known as the Girondins. (François explained to me later that they are named Girondins because many of them hail from the Gironde, which is a region in the southwest.) Now I come to the important part. A huge armed mob marched into the Convention and demanded the arrest of the Girondins. Some of them managed to escape – to Caen, where they have followers too. It is bad news if the moderate members of the Convention have been expelled. But François – to whom I showed the paper – is full of hopes that they will manage to stir Normandy into outright rebellion against the Convention, like other areas that have rebelled to the west and south. In his opinion a noose is tightening around the Convention's neck. If it brings an end to the Revolution, and with it our confinement I would be so happy. But Normandy is not far away, and I am not sure I want to find myself in the midst of a civil war.

Château de Vaillegard, 2 July 1793

François is impatient for news but we have had none since Gregoire brought the newspaper. I think he is hoping that someone will come to tell us that a civil war has begun. I fear that if it did he would run away to join it. He finds it even harder than me to endure our confinement.

I am doubtful that anyone would be able to stir up civil war here. It is so quiet. Sitting at the open window all I can hear is a cow low in the far field! It is only a day's journey by carriage from the château to Paris yet it feels as if the city is a hundred leagues away.

I dream of the time when we can return to Meudon and our friends will return home. I miss them. I miss how my life used to be. We have been here for three months. Three months! I can scarce believe that is all. It feels more like three years.

Château de Vaillegard, 10 July 1793

I am not allowed outside now, as the fields are full of villagers, bringing in the harvest. François let me look through his spyglass and I could see men and women in the far field, loading the wagons with hay. I would like to run downstairs and across the field to watch them. How much longer must we stay here? Mama and Papa seem to enjoy our retirement. She sews, Papa reads and in the evenings they play chess or piqué until it grows too dark to see. Mama has still not touched the fortepiano.

I have just asked Papa when we will go home, and he says that we *are* at home! He does not understand how I feel. He loves this place, the quietness of it. It is home to him, but it will never be home to me. Meudon is my home. Will we never return there? I don't understand why we must stay here. How can it be safer than Meudon, if we even have to hide? I said so to François and he told me that I was being stupid, and then we quarrelled.

Château de Vaillegard, 14 July 1793

François has just been in to see me. I was reading and not pleased to see him. To Papa's sorrow, I have never shown much interest in books, but here there is not much else to do but read. And in books I find I can escape into another world, one in which I can live, if only in my imagination.

He had news, he told me. Then he leant over me and whispered – as if it was too secret to be spoken aloud – "Marat has been murdered!" Marat! I remembered that name. Was he not one of the men behind the massacres in Paris last September? I closed my book and sat up at once. The murder was carried out by Charlotte Corday, a young Norman noblewomen from Caen. She went all on her own to

Paris, to murder him. She gained entrance to Marat's house and stabbed him in his bath with the knife she had bought for the purpose. The Girondins' enemies in the Convention believed that the murder was part of a Girondin conspiracy but she insisted that she had acted alone. I wonder why she did it? Did she think that by murdering Marat she would bring to an end all that was bad about the Revolution? She could not escape, but it seems she did not even try to. What courage! And now she is to be executed. All the wrong people are being killed in this Revolution.

Papa confirmed the news but said he wished I had not heard about it. He fears that it will make Marat into a martyr and that will be that. A gesture in vain. But I cannot stop thinking about Charlotte Corday. Such courage to be shown by a young woman.

Château de Vaillegard, 2 August 1793

I am upset. Gregoire is picking vegetables every day, but there is barely any more food on our table. I cannot believe that he has to send all the vegetables to the town. But that is what Jeanne insists. This evening when her swollen legs had borne her upstairs with our meal I said how wonderful their vegetable garden was. I can see from my window how well everything is growing, I added and stared hard into her face. It was as expressionless as usual. She replied what a shame it was that it all had to go to the town!

It is a lie! The vegetables do NOT all go to the town. When I went downstairs earlier I passed by the kitchen. The door was open and I glanced in. It was overflowing with food. Jeanne was scraping carrots, and there were beans and fruit on the table next to her. None of them have arrived on our table. We pay them handsomely for our food, and I swear that they are pocketing the money.

I have told Mama what I saw. She sighed and said that there is not much we can do. She reminds me that our being here has created much extra work for them and that they have shown us much kindness. It is as if we are their servants, in their home, when it is the other way round! If only we could leave. Is there truly nowhere else we can go? How is it safer for us to be here? If we cannot trust them about this how can we trust them about anything else?

François said he always thought they were untrustworthy. Then why did he not say so to me? In future I will take care not to say anything in front of them that I could not say in front of a mob of rioting sans-culottes in Paris.

Château de Vaillegard, 5 August 1793

The Queen has been taken to another prison, called the Conciergerie. I wonder if anyone will try to free her, but it will not be easy for her to escape. She is bound to be heavily guarded. I have not thought about the royal family for a long time. If I feel like a prisoner here, how much worse it must be for them. Her little son – François declares that he is our King now – had already been separated from his mother and sister. And now both children are all alone.

Château de Vaillegard, 7 August 1793

Mama sat down at the fortepiano this evening. I was so pleased – until she began to play. Some of the keys stuck and even Papa could tell it was out of tune. After playing a few bars of a Bach sonata she stopped, her hands still resting on the keys. Poor Mama. She looked so sad. I got up and went to sit beside her. I laid my head against hers.

Château de Vaillegard, 8 August 1793

I am so hungry, my stomach keeps gnawing at me. So as soon as I was allowed out I went to find Gregoire, who was working in his beloved vegetable garden. He straightened up when he saw me and I said how lovely it all looked, how proud of it he must be, and what a shame it was that all the vegetables had to go to the market. He looked at me as if he could not believe what I had just said. So it is Jeanne, who keeps our food back. How does she manage to hide this from him? I wonder if Gregoire will say anything to her. I wonder if any vegetables will appear on our table today!

We have just finished the best meal we have had since leaving Meudon. And I have an idea that all our meals will be more plentiful now.

As well as our usual fare a scattering of late beans and a few carrots appeared on our plates at dinner. Everyone but me looked astonished but Jeanne said nothing, served us silently as is her way. I resolved not to gloat over her discomfiture, but her face as usual gave nothing away. If she is angry, she does not show it.

Château de Vaillegard, 20 August 1793

I am so frightened. Each night now I go to bed wondering
if I will wake to hear the shouts of peasants outside, or the
crackle of flames in my chamber. There has been a decree
ordering all fortified châteaux and castles to be destroyed.
We do not know how vigilantly the decree is being carried
out but are keeping careful watch in turn. I pray that no
one comes here to destroy our château. What would we do?
Where would we go?

Château de Vaillegard, 21 August 1793

I walk about as if I am in a bad dream. Yesterday I was afraid
that our home would be burnt down about our ears. Today
my whole life feels as if it is crumbling about me.

We are to be detained. All of us. I, Isabelle, and all my
family are to be put in prison! An order has come from the
local authorities that every priest and noble in our area is to

be detained. Every single one of us. Why? What are we guilty of? How can we *all* be guilty? And, how did they even know that we were here? Has someone betrayed us? I can imagine who *that* would be. Oh, why do we not hide? Or flee, while we still can. Why must we accept our fate so easily?

I have just crept back up the stairs from visiting the dungeon. It is filthy but I managed to wash the dirt off myself before anyone saw me and asked where I had been. I went down after lunch as soon as Gregoire and Jeanne had returned to the servants' quarters. It was even more horrible than François said and so dark that I could not even see my hand in front of my face. I had to feel my way with my fingers. I could never hide there. Just one thing gives me hope. I discovered a passage, which may be a secret route out of the château. I was too scared to venture down it alone, but I will tell François what I have discovered so we can explore it together.

Château de Vaillegard, 22 August 1793

This afternoon a troop of soldiers and National Guards rode up to the château. My heart turned over inside me when I saw them. But they had not come to escort us to prison. For now we are to be kept here, under guard.

Papa has been given the rules of our detention. I thought we would be kept inside, but we have been given permission to walk in the park, so long as we keep within 100 paces of the château. They need not fear. I will not go anywhere near as far as that with those armed men wandering about. François is haughty in front of them, which does not help.

I have a secret! I hug it close to me. There is *one* place that is not guarded! The old mill. Ha! They would ring it with guards if they knew what lay inside it – the exit of our secret passage. François and I found it this morning when we explored the dungeon.

I hated walking along that passage. I fancied I could hear the despairing cries of the ghosts of long-forgotten prisoners and jumped every time I heard something scuttle. Unlike in the wine cellar at Meudon, the passage started to rise up after we had been walking along it for a while. The ceiling got lower too so we had to stoop and then it got too narrow to walk side by side. I held on to François's jacket as we shuffled forward step by cautious step.

Suddenly I heard François curse. He had bumped full into what felt under our fingers like a wooden door. We had reached the end of the passage, but what an effort it was to open that door. We tugged and pulled in turn at the iron bolt that secured it. So much rust crumbled off it that I was afraid that it would fall apart in our hands. But at last the door swung slowly back towards us. "I will go first," said François. We were talking in whispers. I do not know why, for no one could possibly have heard us.

We crept forwards, me so close behind François that my nose was almost pressed into his jacket. The air felt fresher here, though it was still dark. I couldn't think where we were. Gradually the dark lifted until I found I could see the outline of François's back. As it lifted more I realized where we were. In the old mill!

We walked carefully around the rooms. It is half a ruin. No one can have lived here for a long time. All the way back we talked about it eagerly. I am cheered to know that we have found a way to escape – though I am not looking forward to going back into that passage!

Château de Vaillegard, 23 August 1793

As soon as I woke this morning I remembered all that had happened yesterday. I lay there thinking about it – the arrival of the guards, and the secret passage we'd found in the dungeon. I lay there so long that Mama came to my room to ask if I was ill.

François was still excited about our discovery, but I picked at my breakfast glumly. Yesterday I had felt confident that we could escape. I don't feel so confident now. What would we do when we had escaped? Where would we go? How would we live? We have no papers, and precious little money. François vanished into his room as soon as breakfast was over. When I walked past, the door was shut. I opened it slowly. François looked round quickly. "François," I began. "I must talk to you." He smiled, as if he already knew what I was going to say. "We cannot escape. Where would we go? How would we live?" He was silent. "Please," I pleaded. "Do not do anything rash." Still he said nothing, but I knew he had made up his mind. I will never change it. He is so stubborn. He held out his arms and we hugged each other. I did not say anything more, just held him tight.

Château de Vaillegard, 24 August 1793

François has fled. Gone in the night, as I knew in my heart that he would. I found a letter tucked under my bolster when I woke. He must have come into my room and put it there when I was asleep. It merely said that he was sorry, but he could not stay. He had gone to fight. He prayed that we'd understand and forgive him. It was carefully worded in case it fell into the wrong hands.

I took it to Mama and Papa. I put it into their hands without a word. Mama was quite unable to speak. She sank into a chair, her face white. Papa was bewildered. "How could he escape the guards?" he said. I said nothing. How would it have helped to tell them about the secret passage? Nor was I sure he had even taken that route. It might have been possible to leave by the window. Would any of our guards have noticed? They are drunk much of the time. They raided the cellar the day they arrived and have helped themselves since to whatever they please. Last night their carousing kept us all awake till late. Some of the guards are downstairs now, in the vaults. They say they are searching for François, but it is a mere pretence.

Château de Vaillegard, 28 August 1793

Our guards have been changed and orders regarding our detention have got stricter – as I discovered this morning when one of the guards pointed his pike at me. I backed away fast, terrified by the menacing way he was waving his weapon about. And I had not walked even fifty paces from the house.

Papa was outraged. "Put your pike away," he said. "She is but a child." For once I did not protest that I was not. The guard muttered something rude, but at least he lowered his pike and I could breathe again. Mama hopes that we will be allowed to remain here, under guard – but I fear her hope is a slender one now that François has run away. Papa has had to answer so many questions about him. The guards are very angry and amuse themselves by taunting us about his likely capture, which upsets us all. It is plain they do not believe he has run away to fight in the republican army any more than we do! I feel proud of him.

I have learnt why we are detained. All the châteaux in this area have been visited by the Commissioners of the Committee of General Security and all nobles residing in them told to hold themselves under detention – as suspects. But what we are suspected of I cannot imagine! And no one has told us.

Château de Vaillegard, 30 August 1793

Our guards look at us curiously – as if they have never seen an aristocrat before. Gregoire says that some of them live in nearby villages. They must truly hate us to choose such a task.

I took Wolf outside this morning and walked him up and down, keeping close to the house and ignoring our captors as best I could. Gregoire has promised to take him on a proper walk later – if he can persuade Wolf to go without me.

Château de Vaillegard, 5 September 1793

Now that I am a prisoner I often find myself thinking about the Queen and her poor children. How grateful I am that I have not been separated from my parents. It is over a year now since the royal family were imprisoned. What must it be like to be in prison a whole year?

Another detachment of soldiers and officials arrived here today. They are downstairs now, making a list of our possessions. I hated to see how they fingered everything. One of them knocked over a precious china ornament. When I heard it smash I was so upset that I ran upstairs to my room. Is everything we have to be seized by the Republic? Are we not to be tried first – or have they already made up their minds that we are guilty? I have hidden what I can. I have stitched my jewellery, money and the buckle into the hem of my travel gown. I have not decided what to do about my diary. I sleep with it now under my bolster.

I am reluctant to destroy it. It is my memoir of my past life. And to write in it gives me what little comfort I still have. One day if I marry and have children I will show it to them, and they will learn what it was like to live through a revolution. I long for the day when I am able to look back and say, it is over. Oh, will that day *ever* come? But I am in terror thinking what would happen if my diary should come to the notice of our guards. At a single stroke we would be transformed from mere "suspects" into the accused and placed under arrest.

Château de Vaillegard, 6 September 1793

The war is going badly for the Republic. "Oh, I am sad to hear that," I said untruthfully, as loudly and clearly as I could so that Jeanne would hear me. Our gaoler – for that is how I think of her – had just lumbered up the stairs with a tray, on which were portions that would barely keep a mouse alive. My words must have surprised her for her face actually showed for once how she felt. She looked startled as if it was the last thing she expected me to say.

Beauvais prison, 1 October 1793

I write this sitting on a stool, in one corner of my narrow cell, huddled over my page, so that my cellmate will not see what I am doing. I had not thought I would have to share with another. It is not going to be easy to keep up my diary. My cellmate is a cobbler's wife from Senlis. She seems kind, but she says little. She has not told me why she was brought here. I don't think she knows. If I must share a room, I wish it could be with the girl in the room next to mine. She looks about the same age as me. I saw her enter it before we were locked in. We smiled shyly at each other.

I never expected to be imprisoned in a convent! All the nuns have left, are in hiding or fled, or in prison themselves. But there is a chapel where we can pray. We will go there tomorrow. The air here is very bad. A horrible smell rises up from the gutter below my window. I pray it does not make us sick.

The sun is sinking now and it will soon be too dark to write. At least I assume it is sinking. I cannot see it. Little light enters this narrow cell.

I have yet to pass a night here. We arrived in the afternoon. As I was passing by the window earlier today I saw a small party of National Guards ride up the drive to the château on horseback. I felt sure I knew why they had come – and I was right. The official in charge informed us that we were to be taken that very day to Beauvais, to be imprisoned in the convent there. When he confirmed that we were *all* to go, I felt so frightened. Mama flung herself on her knees and implored him not to take me too. Papa joined his entreaties to hers. "She is but a child," they said. "She has done nothing wrong." But the official merely said that all the family were to be housed in Beauvais. He had a face like stone, and a heart like one, not to be moved.

Mama helped me pack. While her attention was elsewhere I tore some blank pages out of my diary and slipped them inside my bodice. I was in a quandary about what to do about my diary. I did not dare take it with me. So I resolved to burn it. I lit a fire in the grate and threw it in. But as soon as a little flame began to curl round the pages I reached in and seized it back and blew on it hard to put it out. I brushed off the charred pages. No, I could not bear to burn my diary. Some memoir of my past life must remain. I emptied my jewellery box, and laid it inside. Then I turned the key to lock it so that even if the box is found no one will be able to open it. I took it out to the garden. When none of our guards was looking, I dug a little hole and laid it inside. I patted the earth down firmly. Then I made a promise to myself. One day, when the Revolution is over, I will come back and find it. I will survive this travail. I *will*.

As we drove away I gazed and gazed at the countryside. I had grown mightily tired of looking out onto fields and woods, but now, what I would give to be able to look on to them rather than the stone walls of my prison. All I can see from my window is grey. So, farewell, blue skies. Farewell, green fields. And farewell, my little Wolf. I am trying not to think about Wolf. I was miserable to part from him. Gregoire has taken charge of him. He whispered to me before we left that he would take greatest care of him until I can return to claim him. I felt too sad to speak, but I pressed his hand gratefully. Oh, Wolf. I miss you most awfully.

Beauvais prison, 2 October 1793

I have passed my first night in prison. I slept on sacking. It was so uncomfortable that it was a long time before I could sleep. My cellmate had no such trouble. I lay there, listening to her snores.

It was a horrid awakening. At first I could not think where I was. I stretched out my hand, feeling for Wolf. He was not there. The cobbler's wife was muttering to herself in the bed next to mine. Slowly what had happened came back to me. I was in prison. Outside I could hear the turnkey's gruff voice and the rattle of keys in the lock. Up and down the corridor I heard doors open and slam. As I made my *toilette* I wished there was a curtain between our beds. Oh! Someone approaches. I must stop writing.

I can breathe again. It was only Mama. Even so, I hid my writing away until she had left, in case she asked about it. She has made me chocolate, which has heartened me. I offered some to Cécile, the girl who is kept in the next room. She shares it with an elderly nun, who Cécile says spends most of her time on her knees praying. Her parents are in a cell at the other side of the cloisters. They are nobles like us. I am glad that my parents are not so far away. But, she says, they can wave to each other! She seems quite resigned to our imprisonment.

I do not know how long we will stay here. But it is not as bad as I'd feared. We are a motley bunch – there are nobles, priests, nuns, servants and many ordinary people. I cannot understand why they are here. They look like good people. Some are very poor. The very people the Revolution was to help are in prison! When I see how poor they are I feel ashamed of my past life. It is no wonder that we were so hated. We had so much and they have nothing. The worst inmates are our guards. They sing revolutionary songs and drink and swear so loudly that we cannot help but hear what they say. Their language makes us blush. To think that such creatures have charge of us.

Beauvais prison, 10 October 1793

The days pass so slowly. I wish I had thought to bring something to do. Cécile has her embroidery and has lent me some of her books to read. But I cannot attend to anything for long. I dearly wish I could distract myself from the thoughts that torment me. I cannot stop worrying about François – is he safe, or has he been captured? Mama and Papa have not mentioned him once since we came here, but I do not doubt that they are as anxious about him as me.

On one of my precious pieces of paper I have drawn a picture of Wolf from memory. As I cannot colour it, I have shaded it, using a piece of burnt wood. I am quite proud of it. It is a good likeness. I showed it to Cécile. She burst into tears. I was taken aback – she is usually so composed. I begged her to tell me what had upset her. She explained that she had a dog too, Bonbon, who she misses awfully. She described him to me. Indeed we spent so long describing our dogs and talking about them that I feel I know her dog almost as well as I do Wolf. I offered her paper so that she could draw a picture of her dog too. But she says she cannot draw at all. So I will try and draw a likeness of him for her.

Beauvais, 15 October 1793

Our gaolers are rejoicing. Queen Marie Antoinette was executed yesterday. I refused to let our guards witness my distress and went back to my room to shed tears. Our poor Queen! At least her sufferings are over, but I feel so for her children, now both fatherless and motherless.

Beauvais, 20 October 1793

The nun heard my confession in chapel today. It is a long time since I have made confession, and I feel better for it. She whispered that one of the priests has smuggled in consecrated wafers and if we would like, will give us communion. It is very brave of him. He is sure to be punished if they are discovered. As I walked slowly back to my room I found myself thinking about our dear priest. What his fate was, we never learnt.

Returned from my dreary daily trudge around the cloisters with Mama to find Gregoire had come by with clothes for us, and news for me that Wolf does very well. He is kind but I had a lump in my throat as he told me about the walks they take together. Oh Wolf, have you forgotten me already? I felt a bit tearful when he left for Mama will not let him return. She is afraid that he is putting himself in danger by showing us such care and loyalty. Some of the other prisoners have had less welcome news I fear. So many people are being imprisoned. And there is a rumour that we will soon be leaving here. I hope that wherever we are sent we are kept together. I could not bear to be parted from Mama and Papa.

Beauvais, 22 October 1793

A wagon left today for Paris. I heard one prisoner murmur that if he is transferred he will try to escape. I have finished my drawing of Cécile's dog. She smiled when I showed it to her. She says it is just like him!

Chantilly prison, 26 October 1793

Arrived by wagon this morning at the château of Chantilly – our new prison. What a blessed comfort it is to write that we are all here – Mama, Papa and me. Not everyone was transferred and I was very afraid that I would be left behind at Beauvais.

We had little time to make ready for our journey. In the morning we were shown papers informing us of our transfer, and at night we were bundled into the wagons that were to take us to Chantilly. I pray I never have to undergo such a journey again. We left late at night but did not arrive until 11 in the morning! The cart I sat in stank, and jerked and jolted its way through every pothole till I ached all over, and when we rattled through a very big one a poor person was thrown forwards on to the muddy straw lining the cart and cutting his chin. Mama wiped it for him with her handkerchief. We had to pass through towns and villages and in some of them people came out of their houses to watch us go by. I had rather they had stayed inside. They jeered at us – as if we were wicked criminals. Oh, the humiliation! It upset me very much. I huddled as close to Mama as I could and laid my head in her lap to shut out their jeers. National Guards escorted our wagons. We could not go very fast for some of them marched on foot next to us. One young one kept glancing at Cécile. In the moonlight I swear I saw her blush but she looked away quickly. I am not surprised that he admires her. She is very pretty.

We drove through the gates of the château of Chantilly, our new prison, in the morning. Such confusion there was! Mattresses, bundles, everything was simply hurled out of the wagons into the courtyard. When Papa tried to find ours, he was told that we would have to wait until they were sent up to us in our rooms. I am sure they mean to rob us. I am mightily relieved that my jewels and gold coins are stitched into the hem of my gown.

Once we had climbed out of the wagons we were herded into the chapel of the château. Mama was shocked to see that it was being used to store flour. Sacks of it were piled up everywhere. I perched on top of one of them. My legs were sore and bruised from being knocked about in the wagon and I did not care where I sat down. We were scarcely all in when two officials marched in, tricolour sashes draped across their shoulders, to read the roll call. One of our gaolers, whose name I did not hear, bawled insults every time a noble's or priest's name was read. Our nun bore this calmly –

she is a saintly person. I clung to Mama's hand. I was mightily relieved when we were taken to our cells. I at once fell asleep on the chair.

Chantilly, 27 October 1793

It is most peculiar to be imprisoned in a château. Its owner, the prince de Condé, fled France soon after the Revolution began and the big château, built in the sixteenth century, has been pulled down, which makes me feel very sad. Our prison is in what is known as the "petit château".

I am fortunate. I have a nicer view from my window than I did in Beauvais though I wish that Mama and Papa's cell was nearer to mine. I share my room with a farmer's wife. Our room is on the third floor and I can look out at the forest, and the gardens that surround the château. There are moats too. We cannot go into the gardens, but we are allowed to walk in the courtyard, or on the terrace outside the window, always under the watchful eye of our guards. We are even able to go up to the gate and talk to those outside. Our guards look askance at this and whisper among themselves. I wonder how long it will be before that privilege is denied us. Mama urges me to keep away from it. She says we must try to be good prisoners and obey the rules. I will do my best. If they see that we are good and obedient it may be that we will be released sooner. I still do not understand why I am here, but Cécile, who I saw in the courtyard earlier today, says that we must be here because we are all suspects. I said, what are we suspected of? She does not know, but whispered to me that she had heard that a new law was brought in late in September. It is called the Law of Suspects. In this law all aristocrats, even the children of aristocrats, are suspects! I was puzzled. "How can that be?" I said. "We were imprisoned in August, even before this law came into being!" She shrugged.

I am sorry for Cécile and her parents. They are all in one big room. It must hold full 25 people, of all ages. Bawling infants, young children, old men – all are herded together. When the mattresses are down, there is barely room to move. Cécile says they pile up the mattresses each morning. I felt quite upset but Cécile accepts this as gracefully as she does everything.

Chantilly, 30 October 1793

It is odd. Mama and Papa behave almost as they did before the Revolution. It is as if they are trying to pretend that we are not in prison at all. There are quite a few aristocrats imprisoned here and they all make calls, and meet together in the evenings to play cards and talk. I have even heard the pianoforte being played! I was afraid that we might have been shunned because of Papa's past support for the Revolution and because he was still a deputy at the time of the Paris massacres. But everyone is very kind.

Do I make my prison sound almost pleasant? Then I will explain that I am trying not to dwell on its worst aspects. I am slowly getting used to those. The best is that there are many girls and boys about my age to talk to. We are all prisoners now so it cannot matter what I say. The boys find confinement especially hard. They need to run about more than we girls do, and the only place they can do this is in the courtyard, which annoys some of the older prisoners. Some mothers have even brought in their babies to nurse. Mama was shocked that so many bring in such young children. She would never have done such a thing. But I can understand I think. It must be very hard to be parted from your babies.

Chantilly, 1 November 1793

I have had my first potato. Jeanne was right about them. They are disgusting. How can the English eat them? It was hard and lumpy and had bits sprouting out of it. All our food is awful. It is a wonder more of us don't fall sick. I think about food nearly all the time. I am so hungry that my stomach often hurts. Last night I dreamt that I was sitting at a table, which was dressed for a banquet. All manner of delicacies were laid before me. I picked up my knife and fork to take my first mouthful and – I woke up! I felt hungrier than ever and so miserable.

Chantilly, 6 November 1793

I have made an extraordinary discovery. Cécile is Armand's cousin! I learnt this while telling her about my dream. In my dream I'd escaped, by climbing out of the window on to the terrace outside. I was heartbroken to wake and find myself still in prison. I find my confinement harder and harder to bear. I confided my dream to Cécile. But Cécile does not share my longing to escape. She shook her head. "I could never leave Mama and Papa," she said. I asked if she had any other family in prison. She said she did not think so, but that there was one cousin whose whereabouts she did not know. "He escaped from Paris after the massacre of the Swiss guards," she said. "A family near Paris hid him and helped him to get home." I was so startled that I could not speak. I sat and stared at Cécile. I was silent so long that she asked me what ailed me. "Armand," I whispered at last. "Armand de Beauvantes – he is your cousin?" Cécile nodded, astonished. "Was it your family who hid him then?" she exclaimed. "Oh, thank you, thank you!" We cried and hugged each other. "For what you did, I will always think of you as a sister," she said. She told me that his family had an estate in Normandy and a house in Paris too. And she has told me where it is. I dare not write down the address, but I *know* that I will not forget it.

Chantilly, 10 November 1793

A lady has complained about her lodging – and has been marked in the gaol book as a troublemaker! Mama has again warned me to be very careful what I say and whom I speak to, and to make sure I obey all the rules. This is not easy, as they change constantly. I feel sure that this is to make it easier for us to break them. It's as if our gaolers want to get us into trouble! I am sad because I dare not talk openly to anyone any more – except to my parents and Cécile, who has become a firm friend. I cannot even trust all the prisoners. There are spies, even here in prison. One prisoner, a count, offered me some of his food. He said he saw that I was hungry and that it saddened him to see such a young girl in prison, and did I have any brothers or sisters. I thanked him and I was about to tell him that I had a brother when I saw how attentively he was looking at me and I lied. And I hate to lie. I said I had no brothers or sisters, and turned my head away quickly, so that he would not see that I was blushing. I will go hungry before I betray anyone – least of all my brother.

Cécile says the count has talked to her as well – asking her all sorts of questions about her family. She does not trust him either. And this afternoon I saw him talking in a corner to one of our warders. It is awful to think that there are those amongst us who would betray us to the keepers in the hope of gaining their freedom.

Chantilly, 5 Frimaire Year II

We have learnt that we have a new calendar. It dates back to the beginning of the Republic – in September last year. What was once the month of November in the year 1793 is now Frimaire, Year II!

All the months and days are named after natural things. The months have names that describe what they are usually like. This will help me remember them. So that is why this month, a frosty one, is to be called Frimaire.

Each month is to be thirty days long, I am told. And each week, the "*décade*", will consist of ten days. Each day will be divided up into ten hours. They will be very long ones then!

I cannot think that everyone will be pleased. For the day of rest will now be every tenth day. Sunday has been abolished. All saints' days have been abolished too. Our poor priests – what must they think!

Chantilly, 13 Nivôse Year II

I am amazed to find myself still alive. Last night, at around ten o'clock, a great hullabaloo met our ears – drums beating, orders bellowed. I could see nothing from my window, which faces over the gardens, so I rushed out of my cell and found a group of prisoners huddled together in the corridor. "What is happening?" I cried. "Cannon are pointed at the château," someone said. The farmer's wife had followed me down the corridor. At these words she broke into a great wail. "We are to meet the same fate as the prisoners in Paris," she cried. Could such a fearsome end be in store for us? Terrified though I was I was determined to find out if it was true. I pushed my way close to a window that faces over the courtyard. The noise was even worse here.

As I peered down I saw that the great entrance gates to the château had been flung wide. A troop of men and women were marching round the courtyard, brandishing torches. Round and round the courtyard they marched, dancing and singing, the heavy cannon they were dragging behind them rattling over the cobblestones. The words of "Ça Ira" drifted up to me. "String them up, the aristocrats. String them up"

– the words Gaspard had sung long ago in Meudon. Those words … that cannon. The farmer's wife was right. We were doomed to die this night! My legs wobbled and I'd have fallen if someone had not taken me by the arm.

Neither the farmer's wife nor I slept that night – I lay there, listening to her sobs, waiting for the cannon to fire, expecting every minute to hear a great boom, to feel the building shudder. I longed for Mama to comfort me. I wished that she was in the room with me. I do not want to die.

In the morning we learnt that revolutionary guards have replaced the National Guards. It was they who we saw marching around the courtyard last night. After what we witnessed, I fear that their arrival bodes ill for us.

Chantilly, 18 Nivôse Year II

We have had orders that our meals are to be taken in the gallery. So when the bell rang for dinner today I made my way down there, clutching the basket in which I keep my goblet and cutlery. Guards stood sentinel around the room. An officer and some officials marched round the tables. I expect they thought they looked important. It was most disconcerting. We had to sit exactly where we were told, but there are too many of us to all eat at once, and I had to wait until the first prisoners had finished. Our fare is no better – and there is hardly enough of it to hold body and soul together. Today: salted water with bits floating in it (they call this soup). I have no idea what followed it – it was like nothing I'd ever eaten before. Even Wolf would have refused it. The guards never took their eyes off us, so I tried to swallow the disgusting stuff. It made my stomach heave.

We sit at three tables – I at a table with the other families. Another table is reserved for unmarried men and priests. The third is occupied solely by those who are here on their own. I was somewhat startled to see a married lady there. She did not touch her food, but stared vacantly ahead as if she did not know where she was. I later learnt that her husband had been taken away to Paris, and her pleas to join him were refused. Our commissioner – a man named Martin – has no heart.

Chantilly, 3 Pluviôse Year II

More and more prisoners are being transferred to Paris. But the prison is as full as ever. Almost as soon as one wagon train has departed another arrives, full of suspects. Sometimes it feels as if half of the country must be either in or on its way into captivity. *Why* are so many people being put in prison? When will this awfulness end? I often think about my brother and Armand. I pray that they are still at liberty. Sometimes I find myself wishing I had run away with François, and at liberty myself. Liberty! Was there ever a sweeter word?

Chantilly, 15 Pluviôse Year II

If only we had news! We are not allowed to write letters and the only news we have is what we can obtain from new inmates. They tell us that bad things are happening in Paris. Each night I pray on my knees that we are not sent there.

I have had such a fright! I fell asleep while writing and was woken by the rasping of the key in the lock. The turnkey stood back to let the warder in. Our room was to be inspected. I had barely time to stuff the page I had been writing up my sleeve. Fortunately they did not see, or I'd have found myself on the next wagon train for Paris.

I must write more sparingly – and save what paper I have. I am growing woefully short of paper and ink.

Chantilly, 2 Ventôse Year II

I simply have to write today. Papa was taken away from us last night and sent by wagon to prison in Paris. Mama's grief has quite prostrated her. Nothing I say gives her comfort. I am tired from weeping and cannot write more.

Chantilly, 15 Germinal Year II

I can hardly bear to write this and my tears fall faster than I can write. I am to go to prison in Paris! Without Mama! The warder summoned me and was deaf to Mama's and my pleas to leave me here, or to send her too. Cruel, cruel man. Such terror fills me when I think what might lie ahead of me.

I have some little comfort, but it is selfish of me to rejoice. I will not be entirely alone. Cécile is coming to Paris with me. She came to my room in tears. I stopped packing to try and console her. Her mama will remain here too. We have not been told where we will be imprisoned. Nor do we know why we are being sent away. What have we done to deserve such a fate? I must be brave, but I feel so afraid. My only hope is that I will be put in the same prison as Papa – though I do not even know which that is. Mama promises me that she will do her utmost to join me as soon as she can.

We tried to keep up our spirits but as soon as Mama had left us we burst into tears again. What is to become of us?

Plessis prison, Paris, 18 Germinal Year II

Of all our three prisons this is the worst! I am desolate to think that I am to be held in such a place. Beside it Chantilly seems a palace! Last night our keeper promised that we would be transferred to a more fitting prison for us than this – which is for counter-revolutionaries and falls under the jurisdiction of the dread President of the Revolutionary Tribunal, M Fouquier-Tinville himself. But it was a lie. We learnt today that we are to stay. We are all – young and old – declared to be troublemakers. Troublemakers! I wept when he told us this. If such lies are to be believed what hope do we have?

Earlier we had been ordered to hand over any scissors or

knives we owned, and all our valuables, jewels and money, except for 30 francs in paper money. I handed over what I had obediently, but I quite forgot what I still had concealed in the hem of my gown! I will not hand that over now.

My single comfort is that I am allowed to write and receive letters and before I slept I wrote a hasty note to Mama on one of my precious sheets of paper. I handed it to the clerk. I pray it reaches her. I know how much she will want to know where I am and that I am safe and well.

I run ahead too fast. I will go back now and recount what I can recall of our journey here.

We left Chantilly on what I think was 16 Germinal – how the new calendar confuses me! – and did not arrive here, at Plessis prison, until early the following day. We sat a full hour in the wagon, in the courtyard of Chantilly prison. What caused our delay I do not know. A chill wind whipped our cheeks. I prayed that there had been a change of heart – that we would find ourselves taken down and returned to our old prison. The horses whinnied impatiently. Commissioner Martin was to escort us. My heart sank when he appeared at last. As he walked towards his carriage one of the horses reared, and the coachman had some ado to bring it under control. Maybe the sight of the commissioner frightened it. But only animals have nothing to fear from this man.

There were several wagons in the courtyard. I was sitting in the first one, Cécile next to me. Our mothers had found room at one of the windows overlooking the courtyard. I kept my eyes fixed on Mama until the gates had shut behind us. I tried not to cry as we passed out of the prison and I could see her no more. I remembered our last embrace, how she had whispered that my safety mattered more to her than anything in this world.

We were surrounded by National Guards. Hateful Martin rode ahead of us in a great berline. It rained and we got soaked for we had no shelter. I was relieved when we drew up at an inn – I am sure this was to rest horses and men and not for our sakes. I felt stiff and sore as I was helped down from the wagon. My hair was dripping wet and I wrung it out as well as I could. At least for a time we had warmth, food and shelter. I was so famished that my poor stomach complained when I chewed on a piece of bread. As I ate I tried to forget how people had stared at us as we drove past. We were quite a solemn procession, drums beating as we entered the towns and villages behind commissioner Martin's stately berline. I kept my head held high. "Remember who you are," I said to myself. "Courage." Not everyone was unkind. In one place I heard a child ask his mother why such young girls were in the wagons. She told him to shush and hurried him back indoors. But before she did so I caught her eye. There was such pity for us in her face that I felt my courage seep away and I had much ado not to cry.

It was past nightfall when we reached Paris. As we waited

at the gates I stared up at the walls. Suddenly a feeling of such dread overcame me. How forbidding they looked. The very stones seemed to mock me. "Ha! You will never escape now."

The street lanterns had been lit and as we trundled forwards again I looked about myself. I could not think where I was. Yet this was the city I once knew and loved so well. Few people were about at this late hour, except for soldiers, and they took little notice of us. Wagons bearing prisoners must be a common sight in the city now.

We drove about for so long that I began to fear that we were lost. We implored our guards to tell us where we were going but they did not seem to know either. At last we drew up at a big dark building. As I stared up at the barred windows I felt myself shiver. Was this fearful place to be my new home? Martin had left us but the official who had charge of us now went up to the gate and knocked. After a time a porter shuffled out, thrust a lantern up at our faces, and told us that there was no room. Our guards muttered among themselves and looked at us grumpily as if it was *our* fault that the prison was full.

My head was drooping when I felt Cécile pinch my arm. I started awake. "Look," she said in a trembling voice. I followed the direction of her arm – and felt fear seep through me. Across the river soared the dark towers of the Conciergerie – the most dread prison in Paris, which few leave unless to climb the steps to the guillotine. Others in the wagons had seen it too and such wails and cries broke out amongst us. Cécile and I clung to each other. Were we to be taken there? I did not look up again until I heard someone cry that we had passed it. What blessed relief that was. If I was not to be locked up there I felt could bear almost anything else.

It was about one in the morning when we drew up outside a building on the rue St Jacques. A porter came out, keys jangling on his vast belly. I heard someone say that we were at the Plessis. It had been part of the university before the Revolution. It felt strange to think that I was to be locked up in a place of learning.

We drove under an archway and halted. A guard helped me down. We walked through several great gates. I trembled at the sight of the huge men lumbering around the yard – our new gaolers. We were ushered – if I could call it that – into a big dark hall and told to wait. I reminded myself that anywhere would be better than the Conciergerie, but as we huddled together on benches I could not help but feel afraid again. One of our gaolers dumped a big bucket of water by our feet. I drank from it thirstily.

Mattresses were brought in and thrown down. I curled up on mine to sleep. I was so tired, but I am sure I'd not have slept so long and well had I known then that we were fated to stay here, in such a fearsome prison.

Plessis prison, 19 Germinal Year II

I have found a safe place to hide my diary. As the roll was called this morning I stumbled and nearly tripped over a loose board in the floor. As soon as I was alone I pulled up the board and to my joy discovered that there is space enough beneath to conceal my diary. No one knows about it – I have not even told Cécile, or the lady with whom I share my cell. She was once at court, and no one could be kinder. Yesterday, I was so weak with hunger that I felt the room swim around me when I stood up to fetch the coffee and chocolate the gaolers had brought for our breakfast. I sat down again, and put my head between my knees. Soon afterwards I felt a soft hand lift my head gently and a goblet of hot coffee was held to my lips. "Drink," a lady's voice said. "It will restore you." I sipped the coffee slowly, feeling it warm me down to my toes. An innkeeper brought up our dinner later – but there was not much of that. Prisoners on the floors below had already helped themselves to most of it.

It is tiny this cell – just room for our two mattresses and two chairs. We have laid the mattresses end to end so that there is room to move about. In the morning we put them on top of each other. It is not very comfortable and I must curl up so that I do not kick the Countess – the lady who brought me coffee this morning. She insisted I sleep near the window. The air in the prison is foul, but it is fresher there. She treats me as kindly as if I were her daughter.

I spend much time at the window. There are bars on it but I can see across the walls of our prison to the spires of churches and rooftops. I try not to look down at the streets. It hurts to see people still at liberty going about their business. But if even innocent people like us are locked up, how long will any of them stay free?

A little bird hopped on to the sill. I kept very still, but he must be used to people, for he stayed there for quite some time watching me. He flew away at last when the door opened and startled him. Dear little bird. I wish I could fly away too.

Plessis, 1 ~~Germinal~~ Floréal Year II

Heartening news! We are allowed to send to our own houses for food. I will write at once to my grandmaman's house. I pray that there is someone there willing to bring it to me. It is considered unpatriotic to help an aristocrat, so I am not very hopeful. Why should anyone risk imprisonment just to help me? Cécile has written to her house already, and has had a reply! I was secretly hoping that Armand would see her letter, and bring in the meal himself. But it is a stupid fancy. How could he take such a risk? Is it even likely that he is in the city – a place so dangerous for aristocrats? But I do wish I knew whom she wrote to. She has not mentioned Armand's name again to me and I feel too shy to ask.

Plessis, 5 Floréal Year II

I have wrapped myself in every garment I possess. It is almost too cold to write. It may be spring, but it is icy in here. My turnkey, seeing that I have more than one gown, actually asked me to give him one of them! I refused and now I am afraid he may try to steal it when "inspecting" my room. I envy Cécile – she has a fireplace in her room. I helped her break up her chair to use as firewood – our gaolers are so drunk that they should not notice – and we fed it into the fire piece by piece. I bribed one of the turnkeys to give us a candle. He brought a wretched stub. There was a bit of loose stone in the fireplace that I struck against the grate to make a spark to light it. Cécile tore a piece of paper from a book and held it to the spark. Such delight I felt as a single flame leapt up. The chair was made of straw and burnt fast. We had to sit very near to the grate to feel any heat at all. I sat so close that I have scorched my gown!

Plessis, 7 Floréal Year II

I was kept awake last night by the crying of the prisoner in the cell next to ours. I could hear the turnkeys talking and laughing outside but not one of them went to her aid. As soon as the bolts were drawn back in the morning, the Countess went to see her. She says she is feverish and has petitioned for her to see the prison doctor. I hope he will come soon. Her cries upset me. I am ashamed to write that I am thinking of me as much as her. We will all get sick if she stays here, crowded in as we are. I have written another letter to Mama. I am careful what I say – the letter is bound to pass through many hands before it reaches her – if it ever does. I have had no response to the note I sent her telling her of our arrival. I wrote that I was well, and had enough to eat. I cannot write that our gaolers show us any care. They do not. Most of them delight in tormenting us. But one of them is kind. I am always relieved when it is his turn to escort us

down to the courtyard for our daily walk. You'd think I'd be
pleased to go into the fresh air, but it is a hateful journey.
We have to pass two by two through great bolted doors on
each floor, each of them guarded by several turnkeys. Every
time we do this it sinks in afresh how impossible it would be
to escape. We walk about, stared at all the time by guards.
I always look up at the windows of the quarter where I am
told the men are imprisoned and wonder if Papa is amongst
them – and if he can see me. I cannot find out if he is here. It
is another small cruelty. We are not allowed to mix with the
men at all. I pity the poor priests most of all. They are housed
in the dungeons.

Plessis, 8 Floréal Year II

My dinner was brought to me today! I fell on it hungrily. It
heartens me to know that there is someone out in the city
who cares enough for me to take such a risk on my behalf.
I shared my meal with the Countess. Her house has been
sealed up and she has no one to send her food. The Countess
explained that they affix seals to prisoners' houses, which
become the property of the Republic. Is it any wonder then
that they lock up so many rich prisoners! I cannot think

why they have not sealed up our Paris house. We had an apartment there, but it was Grandmaman's home. I confess I am surprised that any of the servants still live in the place. We have not had news of Grandmaman for over a year, but I know that she is not in Paris. She never truly forgave Papa for standing in the Assembly, and refused to visit us in Meudon.

I saw the prison doctor today. After he had visited the poor lady in the next cell, he came to our room to talk to the Countess. He wore the red bonnet of a sans-culotte, and has a swarthy complexion and few teeth – as I saw when he smiled at me. He may be a good patriot, but this man knows nothing of medicine. He seems kind though, and promised to write out a certificate for the sick lady. I hope he keeps his word. Promises count for little here. It will allow her to be transferred to the prison hospital. The Countess says he assures her that there she will get better food and care.

Plessis, 1 Prairial Year II

I am all alone in my cell, and am trying not to cry. I have laid out both our mattresses as usual. I am curled up on mine and am pretending that the Countess is lying on the mattress below mine.

But she has gone. My kind Countess has been called to trial and by now will be in a cell at the Conciergerie prison. I had no fear before today that anyone would be called from our corridor – why, I do not know, for the accused mingle here with those of us who are merely suspects – and it came as a great shock when the bailiff came up to our landing and bawled out the Countess's name. I was in Cécile's cell and ran straight back to my room. The Countess had already begun to put her things together. I helped her, wishing there was something more I could do for her. Before she left she told me she would soon return. I burst into tears and she stroked a wisp of hair off my face, took my hands in hers and said that she was innocent of any crime and so had nothing to fear. She was quite composed and I told myself that if she could be so calm then I must be too. She had barely fifteen minutes to make ready and say her farewells.

I ran back to Cécile's room, which overlooks the courtyard, and we watched as the wagon bearing my kind friend and other prisoners lurched forwards. Gaolers ran to open the gate. As the wagon reached it, the Countess looked back, up at the window. She saw me and smiled and I tried to smile back – but I felt my face wobble and I had to turn away. I will never forget her kindness to me. Never, never.

Plessis, 2 Prairial Year II

I cannot bear to see our gaolers. Last night, when the keeper and guards came round to lock up, I shut my eyes tight so they would think I was asleep. I heard steps outside my door, felt the flare of the torch as it was held up to the grating, imagined the turnkey peering in to make sure I had not escaped. One of the dogs was barking, its chain rattling as its master pulled on it, growling at it to hold still – I have never seen such great animals, more like wolves than dogs, more a wolf than my dear Wolf will ever be – but as soon as they had gone, I ran to the door and shook at it and shook at it until my hands hurt and I was quite exhausted.

Plessis, 5 Prairial Year II

Prisoners arrive more frequently now. Several wagons drove though the prison gates today. Dread fills me when I hear the drums begin to beat – the signal the gates are about

127

to open. We had just returned to our cells today when another convoy arrived. It was raining and I was soaked through. I took off my wet gown and rubbed my hair dry on my shawl. Later, in Cécile's cell, I glanced down and saw M Fouquier-Tinville, the public prosecutor, descend from his carriage, and behind him his train of bailiffs, bearing warrants for yet more arrests. Have they not had enough? People are being arrested or sent to the Conciergerie to stand trial for the tiniest things. Sometimes I think about the man Robespierre who people whisper is responsible for the arrests and who it is said hates us all so much that he wants us all to be beheaded. If what is claimed is true and our King was a tyrant, why then we have merely exchanged one tyrant for another. As in Beauvais and Chantilly it is not just aristocrats who are in prison with me. All sorts of people are here who are as bewildered as me to find themselves in prison. One peasant woman has been imprisoned for accidentally standing on a branch of a Tree of Liberty, which, she said, had withered and fallen off. Another stands accused for saying *vive le roi*, but she denies indignantly that she said any such thing. "I am a good Republican," she says – and has collected many signatures to attest to this which she will use for her defence. Her neighbour denounced her – and her neighbour has always hated her, she says.

Cécile has been reunited with her mama! She came on the convoy of wagons that arrived earlier today. I was bitterly upset not to see my mama and am trying to hide from Cécile how I feel. Her mama has been to see me. I had so many questions for her. She says Mama is well. She has brought me a letter from her too, which I could scarcely wait to get back to my cell to read. After I had read it I tucked it into my gown so that I could feel Mama close to me, but now I have put it away with my diary under the floorboard. Mama writes that she is well and endeavouring to be transferred here to be with me. She did not mention Papa.

I miss them so much.

Plessis, 7 Prairial Year II

I am still on my own and find it hard to sleep. It is so noisy in prison. How long will it be before the empty mattress has another occupant? For now, I am glad to be on my own.

Plessis, 10 Prairial Year II

I am writing in my new room. We suspects have been moved
to new quarters in the building opposite – away from those
who have already been accused of some crime – and once
our cells have been unlocked in the morning we can move
about our prison freely, unaccompanied by gaolers. I have
been up- and downstairs about ten times this morning, just
for the joy of being able to do so on my own.

Paris, 12 Prairial Year II

I have done it. I have escaped from prison! My head whirls
when I think back to the moment I knew my chance had
come – a chance that I was sure would never come again. A
uniform lay in a heap half way down the corridor. I did not
hesitate. I picked it up, and ran with it bundled in my arms
back to my cell. I am still amazed that no one saw me. Inside
my cell I flung off my gown, and pulled on the uniform.

My fingers were trembling so much that it took me an age to fasten the buttons. The trousers were too large for me, they were made for a man not a skinny girl like me – so I hoisted them up as high as I could and bound them round my waist with a strip of cloth I tore off my shawl. It was hidden by the jacket that hung down over it. I thrust my hands deep into the pockets and swaggered about the cell imitating the rolling drunken walk of the gaolers. I even found a red cap in one of the pockets.

I lay down on the bed, pulling my blanket up to my chin, and pretended to be asleep. Every time I heard a turnkey's voice outside in the corridor my stomach plummeted and my mind spun in terror. What would I do if anyone came searching for the uniform?

I had no plan. I just knew I had to escape – at least to try. I waited, staring up at the ceiling, the minutes slowly passing, the cell darkening. As soon as the roll had been taken I would leave my cell. When a gaoler came by at last, I lay still, my eyes tight shut. I heard the jangle of keys and a gruff voice enquire what I thought I was doing. "Answer the roll."

"I am sick," I murmured, and prayed that he would leave.

As soon as he had gone I got up and stuffed my gown under my blanket, trying to make it look as if there was someone huddled up in bed. I did not know the hour but I reckoned that I had a full two hours before the keeper came by on his nightly round. I crept to the door and listened.

The corridor was silent, so I pulled on my cap, tucked up my hair under it, allowing some stray locks to straggle down, and then I opened the door quietly and glanced out. The corridor was empty – except for a small group of prisoners who had their backs to me. Taking a deep breath I shut the door as quietly as I could, and crept along the corridor, to the stairs. My heart was hammering inside my jacket. What I was to do now, I did not know. But, I argued with myself, by this hour most of our gaolers are so drunk they can barely stagger. Anyone who sees me will see only my uniform. In such dim light their bleary eyes will not be able to tell that it is a prisoner who wears it!

It was past the hour when the bailiffs come by with the warrants, so I was shocked at the bottom of the stairs to find myself face to face with the public prosecutor, M Fouquier-Tinville, himself. My heart gave a great thump. He had a sheaf of papers in his hands. He stopped and peered at me. "What are you doing here?" he said.

I lowered my voice as much as I could. "I am taking a break from my duties," I growled trying to keep my voice steady.

"Do you know who I am?" he asked.

"Everyone knows the public prosecutor," I answered.

"Do you know where I live?"

I nodded. "I have been there once," I lied boldly. "You yourself sent me."

I do not know what possessed me to make up such a story,

but my answer satisfied him. "Then I'd like you to go there now, and tell my wife that I will not be home until late."

And it was only then that I remembered that I still had to find a way out of the prison! I felt my hands grow clammy. "Yes, but I am not due to go off duty. I am not sure…" my voice tailed away. How could I pass the gaolers at the gate? I'd be stopped – and recognized!

M Fouquier-Tinville snapped his fingers. "Come with me." And so I left my prison, escorted out of it by the public prosecutor himself. "Let this fellow through," he said, as we passed under the archway to the main gate. "He has business to attend to for me."

Not one of the guards stopped me. Who would dare question the orders of the public prosecutor? In a few strides I had left the prison behind me. As I passed through the gates, I felt almost dizzy. I was free. Free! I kept walking, trying to resist the longing to run. It was too soon to rejoice. It was too soon to feel free. How long would it be before the guard whose uniform I'd stolen realized it was missing? What would happen when the keeper did his rounds? Would the bundle of clothes tucked under my blanket convince them that I was asleep? or would they enter my cell? How much time did I have before anyone realized that I had escaped? How soon before they came in search of me?

The street lamps were lit but I kept to the shadows as much as I could. I was still wearing my uniform and no one came up to me. I had not seen my face in a looking glass for many months and felt sure I looked as rough and dirty as any gaoler. Small wonder that I was avoided.

I reached Grandmaman's house. Robert, the porter, was at the gate, lighting a pipe. I walked firmly up to him. How he jumped when he saw me! I must have been a frightening figure – dirty, unkempt, dark hair straggling loose under my red bonnet. He could not have known how scared I was. Would he help me? or turn me away. Could I trust him?

I had no choice. I had to try. "It is me, Isabelle," I said in my own voice.

His mouth fell open. "But how – why…" he stuttered, astonishment writ all over his face.

"I will explain," I said quickly. "But not here. Can I come in?"

He nodded slowly and took my arm, looking about nervously as he did so. "Follow me. I must get you inside before the patrol comes."

I let myself be guided across the courtyard. At the door I hesitated. "Who else is here?" I whispered.

"Only Justine and myself. Mademoiselle, you may trust us."

Justine clapped her hand to her mouth when she saw me, but she asked no questions, merely hurried me upstairs to the attic. "I am sorry for this," she said, as she showed me into a tiny room. "But it is best for now that no one knows that you are here." She brought me a mattress and blankets. "Should the patrol come I will knock three times on your door."

She must have seen how terrified I was because she added quickly: "It is most unlikely that they will, mademoiselle, but it is as well to be prepared." She brought me food – some black bread and cheese. I ate them greedily and I saw a look of pity cross her face. "That poor child," I heard her mutter as she closed the door behind her. "That poor child." At least I do not feel so alone and friendless now. As soon as I have finished writing I will blow out my candle and try to sleep. I have managed to prise open the window a little to let in some air. It is stuffy and airless in this tiny attic room – but after my prison cell I feel as if I am in paradise.

Paris, 13 Prairial Year II

How wonderful it is to feel clean again. I swear that my hair is several shades lighter than it was when I left prison. Kind Justine has been trudging up and down stairs all morning with steaming hot water for me to wash. It took several buckets. I was so dirty. I smelt too. I'd seen how Justine had winced when she put down my bedding last night. She has taken away all my clothes to burn. I am sitting on the mattress, dressed in her second-best gown and clogs!

When I woke I did not know where I was at first. I squinted

at the sun streaming through the tiny window and wondered why there were no bars on it. And why had the gaoler not unlocked my door? When I did at last hear a knock I dived under my blanket in terror. Only when I heard Justine's gentle voice did I dare emerge again.

She brought me hot milk and bread and again I tore at them in my hunger. I have quite forgotten how to be a lady! Justine shook her head and told me to eat slowly.

I told them all that had happened to me. Justine stared at me in wonderment. I said I did not know where to go, but that my feet had brought me here. "And it is right that they did," she said heartily. "Where else should you go, but here? But you must stay in this room for now."

I offered them one of my gold coins to pay for my food. When he saw it, Robert shook his head and told me to hide it. "Put it away," he said earnestly. "It is considered a crime to own gold."

"Is anything not a crime?" Justine muttered. "Is there any one of us that Robespierre does not look upon with mistrust? We are all under suspicion – every one of us. Innocent and guilty alike." Robert shook his head at her. "You may shake your head at me all you like, Robert, but it is true. You know it is, as well as I," she said.

Paris, 17 Prairial Year II

I have been thinking and thinking what to do. I am not as safe here as I thought. Nor do I want to put Justine and Robert in any danger and I am afraid that I have. I must order my thoughts and make a plan. This evening Justine knocked on my door – "Mademoiselle, the patrol is in the street below. They will see your light. Put it out." I was so afraid that my gaolers had come for me that it took three blows before I could summon up enough breath to blow it out. But they did not come in. Justine says I must not be afraid. "They will not come for you now, I feel sure," she reassured me. But, she says, she does not want to draw anyone's attention to my presence here. "We have to write a list of all who live here and post it on the house every day," she said. "We dare not add your name."

Four days have passed now since I escaped from prison but Robert and Justine are just as jumpy as me whenever someone comes to the house. We do not have much food for I share theirs – food is rationed, though Justine says you can eat what you like if you have the money. When she told me that I tried again to give them money for our food but she says it will look odd if they are suddenly seen to dine like kings! Justine goes out each day long before dawn to join the queue at the baker's. But the bread often runs out before she reaches the top of the queue. "The police are supposed to supervise the queue," she told me. "But often latecomers bribe them to put them in front!" She says it is the same at the other shops. "The only people who eat well in this city now are those who still have money and the members of the Convention," she said. "They feast like kings. The rest of us go without. The Revolution has changed nothing," she said to me sadly. "The poor are as poor as they ever were – and everyone goes in fear of his or her life." She told me that the streets are quieter than they used to be. "People are afraid to go out and only go out when they must," she said. I have noticed an odd smell about it too. Paris always was a smelly city, but this is a new smell. One I do not know.

Paris, 19 Prairial Year II

I am writing as fast as I can before my candle goes out. Writing helps to distract me. I am trying not to think where I am. In the light of my candle I can see skulls grinning at me from the walls. Heaps of bones lie scattered about my feet.

Water drips from the ceiling. I am deep below the streets, in the city's catacombs.

I had to flee from Grandmaman's house. It was late in the afternoon when I heard voices outside in the courtyard and then hurried steps mounting the stairs. Three knocks. As calmly and quickly as I could, I wrapped my things in my shawl and opened the door. Robert was standing there, alarm written all over his face. He took my arm. "The guards are here. They are going to search the house. Come – come quickly." He hastened me down the stairs and along a back passage I had never been down before. He pulled up a window. "Get out as fast as you can. Go to the back wall. There is a break in it. Climb over it and make your way along the alley until you come to the street. Stay there. I will come for you as soon as they have gone."

I had one leg over the window frame before he had finished speaking. I was in grave danger. We all were. I could hear Justine protest in the hall. Poor Justine. Poor Robert. How good they had been to me. I could not go back. I must find somewhere else to hide. I put my other leg across the window frame and jumped down. It was not far to the ground and I landed softly. Keeping my head low I ran across to the back wall. I could see where it had partly collapsed. Not daring to look back at the house, I clambered over it and crouched down low behind it so that no one could see me.

I made my way cautiously along the alley to the street.

Once I had reached it I stood up straight, brushing my gown smooth and hoisting my bundle over my shoulder. The streets were quieter than I'd hoped. In crowds you can hide. I tried to look as if I had somewhere to go, and prayed that no one would stop me or follow me. In truth, I was in a panic. Where could I go? Where could I hide? Then a name and address floated into my mind. Armand. "I will always be at your service," he had written to me once, long ago. But was he even here, in the city? I began to look about myself. In my flight I had scarcely observed how fearfully changed the city was. Paris had become a giant workshop! Big buildings like monasteries, convents, schools, colleges – those that had not been turned into prisons – had become workshops and foundries manufacturing guns, cannon and shot for the army. The red glow from forges lit up those public gardens that had not been dug up. Justine had told me that church bells had been removed from church belfries and melted down to make cannon, and cellars even scraped for saltpetre to make gunpowder.

Hammering and banging greeted me everywhere I turned. Many of the street names had been changed. I despaired. How would I even find the street where Armand lived? I felt a stranger in this city. Everything that could remind me that there had once been a king had been destroyed or changed. Statues of kings and saints had been toppled from their plinths. Rude words scribbled on them. It still stank and was as dirty as ever. It was about the only thing about the city that had not changed.

I looked up. I was not alone. A man was staring intently at me. I found that I had wandered into a street so narrow that if I had reached out both arms I could almost have touched the houses on either side. My heart began to thud. I did not like the way he looked at me – as if the word "prisoner" was branded on my forehead. "Do not panic," I told myself. "Be calm." I began to walk swiftly away, but he was across the road in a bound and had my arm in a grip so strong that I could not escape.

"Not so fast," he said.

I tried to twist out of his grasp. "Leave me be," I gasped. "You are hurting me. I have done nothing wrong."

He laughed unkindly. "That's what they all say."

"It is true!" I cried. "I am a good patriot."

"You can tell that to the Commune," he said grimly. "Come along now." What would have happened then had my captor not been distracted by the commotion in the street below I dare not think. A crowd had formed and a guard was shouting to the people to get out of the way. My captor slackened his grip and I managed to pull myself free. I ran down the road and plunged headfirst amongst the people who had fallen back to line the street.

Why had this crowd formed? What had caught their notice? I stood on tiptoe so that I could see over the heads of the people in front of me. A tumbrel, a two-wheeled cart, surrounded by guards was clattering over the cobbles towards us. As it drew level I saw that several people sat inside, their hands tied behind their backs. With a shock I realized that they were being taken to the guillotine. One, a girl, looked barely older than me. That could have been me, I thought suddenly, and a wave of such terror overcame me that I felt quite faint. I'd have fallen if I had not been so squashed in by the crowd. Around me people were jeering and hooting at the prisoners. A man ran behind the cart, hurling rotten food and curses after it. Another did a jig before making a sudden gesture with his finger under his neck. I wanted to shout at them to stop, but dared not draw attention to myself. The girl had bent her head to avoid the filthy missiles. The look on her face, when she lifted it again, was utterly bewildered, as if she did not know why she was there, or what she had done to deserve it.

"A curse on all aristocrats!" someone nearby me spat. I wanted to weep. These people were not aristocrats. They were ordinary people, like those standing next to me. How could they be so cruel? Is that word hurled now at anyone who is hated?

Desperate to get away, I pushed my way to the edge of the crowd, but my captor saw me and with an angry yell was after me again. I flung myself back into the crowd and was swept along with them to the place de la Revolution.

How fitting it was I thought as I fought my way round out of view of my captor that the place named after the Revolution was also the place where prisoners were guillotined. It showed to me the depths to which the Revolution had sunk. The Revolution that Papa had had such hopes for was nothing more now than a merciless executioner. The square was rapidly filling with crowds, come for the day's entertainment – to see the blade fall. The smell I had noticed the day I had fled prison rose from the ground. It was stronger here. Now I realized what it was. Blood. So much had been spilt that here the ground was damp and stained with the stuff. I felt myself retch and held my apron over my nose.

In front of me was the guillotine. I had never seen it before. A platform, on which stood the machine, two upright posts and between them that shining silver blade.

Across from the guillotine a statue of the King's grandfather, Louis XV, had once stood. It had been toppled off its plinth and in its place now was a Statue of Liberty.

In front of the guillotine sat a row of women, all busily knitting and chatting as if it was a public holiday. I too could not drag my eyes away from the scene in front of me. The cart had been unloaded and the first prisoner – a woman – was being helped up the steps to the guillotine. The executioner and his assistant pushed her forward onto a plank and shoved it through the machine. A sort of wooden brace held the neck still. The drums began to roll. The executioner reached for the pulley. I turned away my head and shut my eyes tight.

A cheer told me the deed was done. Another prisoner was being helped up the steps. I could not bear to stay any longer. Using my elbows I pushed my way back out of the crowd. A woman quickly took my place. She looked surprised to see me go. No one else took any notice of me – they were transfixed by the falling of the blade. But as I made my way out of the crowd, a boy's voice whispered in my ear: "You are not wearing a cockade. Get away from this place before you are arrested." I put my hand to my shoulder. The tricolour cockade – symbol of the Revolution – which all patriots wear. I had forgotten! Was that why I had been pursued? "I must have dropped it in the street," I lied. "I will buy another."

I heard a startled gasp. The boy who had spoken leaned forward and gripped my arm. He bent his head and stared hard at me. Utter astonishment was written on his face. I leaned away from him.

"You. What are you doing here?" he whispered. I tried to push him off, but he would not let me go.

"Do you not know me – Isabelle?" he said softly. I shook my head, bewilderedly. The boy was wearing the trousers and red cap of a sans-culotte. How was it this boy knew my name? "Come, we must get away from here," he said. "I will explain. But not here. It is not safe. The city is full of spies."

He bought me a cockade from a little girl on the street

corner and I pinned it to my shoulder. "Follow me," he said. I let myself be led along twisted streets and narrow passages. In truth I had no choice. His grip was too strong. I could not escape. By a ruined church he stopped and pulled me inside. The altar had gone, the pews had been torn away, but I barely noticed. Who was this boy? Why had he brought me here?

"Do you still not know me?" he said. He pulled off his cap. I shook my head slowly. No, and yet there was something familiar about him. The boy put his hand into his pocket and pulled out a handkerchief. He handed it to me. I stared at it. It had my initials embroidered in one corner. "Now do you remember?" he said.

A boy lying on a bed, a sword cut in one leg. Armand.

"You kept it," I said. I felt my lips begin to tremble. Relief that I was no longer alone made me want to cry. He put an arm round my shoulder. I did cry then, the handkerchief tight in my hand.

When I had stopped, he asked me why I was in Paris, dressed like a maid.

"I am in hiding," I said, and I poured out all that had happened to me. Armand listened silently, but I saw him clench his hands when I told him that I had been in prison. He gazed at me in wonder when I explained how I had escaped. "You have the courage of a lion, Isabelle," he said. Then he told me his story. He explained that he had come to Paris to see if he could save his father, but he was too late.

He lost his head on the guillotine soon after he arrived. My eyes filled. Poor Armand.

"Come," he said briskly. "It is almost dark. We must get away from here before the night patrols start."

"I have nowhere to go," I said. "I dare not go back to my grandmaman's house now."

"Nor shall you," he said. "We are going to leave the city." My heart thumped. Leave the city. How I longed to.

"But how can we?" I said. "I have no papers."

"There is a way, but you must trust me," he said.

"I trust you," I said.

"Then follow me." And so he brought me here. It is the safest place he knows. He promised that he would return soon. He has gone for food – he says he knows where it can be found. I did not want him to leave me here, but he was anxious to get me away from the streets. Oh please let him return soon. I cannot bear to be alone in the dark.

A barn, some leagues from Paris

Armand is still asleep, but I woke up when the cows began to low. It gave me quite a fright. So much has happened since I last wrote my diary. Days and nights have got all mixed up in my mind. It is nearly night again now, and when Armand wakes we will leave our hiding place.

I am not even sure where we are. After Armand had returned to the catacombs he led me through them to the limestone quarries outside the city. How we found our way through that dark maze of underground tunnels I know not. Some of the passages were so low we had to stoop to move at all. Others so narrow that we could not walk side by side. At times I felt sure that we were not alone – that others had taken shelter there. Whispers and scuffles broke the silence. Bones crunched under our feet. I held tightly to Armand's hand as he commanded. I knew that if I once let go of it I'd be lost in those tunnels for ever.

Outside the city we made our way to an inn. And there we dined on an omelette. We were the inn's only customers but the innkeeper barely glanced at us. We look like scruffy ragamuffins. "Be bold," Armand says. "Behave as if you have every right to be here. Then we are less likely to be stopped or questioned." His confidence cheers me greatly.

We travel by night and snatch what rest we can by day – in barns, or in ditches. It is not only the revolutionaries and soldiers we have to fear, highwaymen, robbers and bandits plague the countryside around Paris.

My feet ache and ache. I long to soak them in warm water. I'd hoped we could stowaway in one of the barges moored on the river. The Seine flows all the way from Paris

147

to the sea. But the quays are too heavily guarded, Armand says. Besides could we trust the bargemen not to betray us? The fewer people who know about us the safer we are. But my feet protest so much. I can barely hobble. In three more days, Armand thinks, we will reach the coast. Three more days! And then I will gaze on the stretch of water that separates us from England – and freedom! To be free at last – truly free at last. Can such a thing be possible?

Normandy, I do not know the date

I cannot believe that we are here. When I lift my eyes they rest on blue – the blue of the sea! I am sitting on the beach, at the water's edge. I have stretched out my legs on the warm sand and let the waves run over them. The salty water soothes my poor blistered feet. Tonight we will steal away in a fishing boat. I feel sorry for the fisherman, but Armand says he will pay him well to take us across the sea. His pockets are getting lighter now, he jokes. We will have to beg in England. I smiled to myself. In a handkerchief I have jewels and money. I took care not to leave them behind when I left Grandmaman's house.

One thing spoils my happiness – that I leave my family behind. Where are they now? My parents. François. And Wolf.

Has Wolf grown? Thinking about them my eyes blur and I blink away tears. How I wish they were here beside me. I feel guilty – I have abandoned them. In my desperation to escape I thought only of myself. Armand insists I did right. They will be happy to learn that I am safe, he reassures me. We will find them again when it is over, he says. Never fear. One day the people will come to their senses, and Robespierre's reign of terror will end. Then we will go home. Armand is *such* a comfort to me.

England, June 1794

I no longer need to write my diary. My revolution is over. I am safe – safe at last. I can walk where I choose, say what I think. I am free. But before I lay down my pen I must explain how I came to be so – and what happened next.

It had begun to drizzle when we crept over the sands to the fisherman's boat. Waves lapped quietly around it. I balked when I saw it. Was that little boat really to carry us over the Channel? I was thankful that it was not a stormy night. Armand gave the fisherman half the agreed fee. "The other half will be yours when we reach England," he said.

The fisherman held up the coins and growled that it was

not enough. He had refused to accept paper money. "Those assignats – they are worthless. Each day they buy me less."

Armand refused to give him more. I wished he had found another fisherman to take us across to England. I did not like this man's face. I did not trust it. I did not like the way his eyes darted about – mean little eyes that never met ours. But at last he muttered that we could climb aboard. I hoisted up my gown and waded out into the shallow water. Armand, already aboard, helped me climb in. The boat creaked and wobbled as I settled myself down. Armand passed me one of the blankets in the bottom of the boat. "Lie down. Cover yourself. We do not want anyone to see us," he whispered. I crept under the blanket, and lay there, listening to the boat creak and rock. The fisherman was taking a long time to get ready. I pulled up a corner of my blanket to watch. He was fiddling with the sail. Armand lost patience. He whipped something out of his belt – something hard and shiny, a gun! – and pressed the nozzle against the man's leg. "Get on with it," he growled. "Or we will take your boat and you will never see it again."

The fisherman was as startled as I was at the sight of the gun and jumped back. The boat rocked violently from side to side.

"Do not shoot me, citizen," he whined.

"Then make haste, man," Armand said impatiently.

"There is no moon. It is hard to see. Have patience."

I turned to look back at the shore. Even though it was so dark I was sure I could see something – yes, there they were, figures moving silently across the beach towards us.

"Armand," I said urgently. "Look." I pointed to the shore.

Armand cursed and thrust the gun at the man's head. "Have you betrayed us?" he said fiercely.

The fisherman fell on to his knees. "No, citizen. Most assuredly not. Do not shoot me. My family – I have three children…"

"Then haul up the anchor," Armand said. "And be fast about it."

He seized one of the oars and thrust the other into my hands. "As soon as I give the word, row. Row as hard as you can." I gripped the oar, though I had never held one before. I heard the fisherman grunt as he hauled on the anchor. Up the chain came, link by link. There was a splash and with one final grunt the anchor was up and lying dripping in the boat.

"Now!" I dipped my oar into the water. In. Out. In. Out. I pulled on the oar, seeing the beach grow further away. I tried not to think about all that sea surrounding us. It was such a little boat. Over our heads the sail hung limply, but soon the wind caught it and I was able to lay down my oar. Exhausted, I leant forward and watched as Armand pulled in his oar too. He crouched near the fisherman, holding his gun close to him again. "One false move and you join the fishes – citizen," he said.

I felt sure that would be all our fate, if we were even lucky enough to avoid the attention of the men of war patrolling the Channel. But we were fortunate. Not one ship drew close to us.

A brisk wind blew up and tossed us back and forth. Twice I was sick over the side of the boat. By the time the English coast came in sight I no longer cared if I lived or died.

Our adventures were not over. After we had landed and rested we trudged wearily along the beach. I still could not believe that we were truly in England. In the dark had we really crossed the Channel, or had the waves tossed us back to France?

We passed a fisherman. He was whistling as he hauled his boat ashore. As soon as I heard him I knew that we were in England. He told us where we might find food and shelter and before long we found ourselves walking up an English street to an inn. I will never forget what happened then. Everyone fell silent as we walked through the door. The landlord folded his arms and said, in lordly tones: "This is a respectable inn. No vagrants here."

"We are not vagrants," Armand insisted. "I am the count de Beauvantes. And my companion is a marquis' daughter. We seek lodgings and—"

The landlord did not let Armand finish. He slapped down his fist on the table so hard that it shook, and burst into roars of laughter. "If you be aristocrats I be King George of England," he said, wiping tears of merriment from his eyes.

I looked at Armand and then down at myself. At our dirty and salt-soaked clothes. He doesn't believe us. He thinks we are poor refugees who cannot pay, I thought. But we can. I would prove it to him. And so I unwrapped the handkerchief. Next to the gold coins lay a shoe buckle. In the firelight it sparkled on my upturned palm. The landlord fell silent. But I was not looking at him. Nor, I saw, was Armand. "You kept it," he whispered, "all this time."

I quite forgot to be shy. I forgot about the landlord. I forgot that we were not alone. I had no need to conceal anything any more – from him, or anyone else. I was free – truly free at last. I looked into Armand's face. "Yes," I said. "I kept it. I always will."

Historical note

In 1789 France was ruled by a king. His name was Louis XVI. But unlike in Britain, the King's power was absolute. He alone had the power to choose and dismiss ministers. Ordinary people had no say how their country was governed.

Louis, his Queen – the Austrian Marie-Antoinette – and their court lived a life of luxury at the palace of Versailles. But by 1789 the government had run out of money. Something had to be done – not only to put right the public finances but to try and alleviate the sufferings of the people.

In eighteenth-century France most people were peasants, who worked on the land. Though they were very poor they paid most of the taxes. Peasants also had to pay what were called "feudal dues" to their "seigneur" who owned the land they worked. They had to pay to use the seigneur's mill, to work his land, and cross his river. They had to labour on the roads, pay taxes to the state and other taxes called tithes to the church. To make matters still worse, by 1789 the country had had a succession of bad harvests. Winters had been bitterly cold, and summers unusually hot. Food prices rose. But the poor still had to pay their taxes. By the late 1780s the peasants had had enough and began to take matters into their own hands. Starving and desperate, they shot the seigneurs' doves that ate their crops, set traps to catch the game they were not allowed to hunt, and attacked wagons filled with grain.

As part of the efforts to sort out the country's problems, the King asked his people to send their grievances to him. These were known as the *cahiers de doléances*. He also asked the Estates General to meet – a body which had not met since 1614. In the eighteenth century France's people were divided into three "estates" or classes. The first estate was the clergy, the second the nobility, and the third everyone else. Those who were allowed to vote elected "deputies" to represent them in the Estates General. The deputies elected from the Third Estate were mostly middle-class men – lawyers, doctors, journalists, officials. Each estate had a single vote, which made it easy for the first two estates to block reforms proposed by the third. The Third Estate was the biggest and they demanded changes and freedoms that the King did not want to give them. They wanted to be rid of the old regime which burdened the very poorest, the peasants, with taxes they could not afford to pay. They wanted an end to the feudal system. They believed that they, the biggest estate who represented most of the people, should decide how France should be governed, and they called on the other two estates to join them. A number of the richest, more liberal aristocrats agreed with them, as did many of the clergy. But the Queen and the King's brother Artois refused to accept that any power should be devolved to the people. The King himself was a kind man, but indecisive. He was happiest when hunting or locksmithing. Pulled this way and that between the advice of the Queen and his staunchly royalist brother Artois on the one hand and his finance minister, the Swiss Jacques Necker, on the other, he was ultimately powerless to prevent the three estates from forming into one "National Assembly".

Throughout the summer of 1789 ferment in Paris bubbled away. Agitators met at the coffee houses of the Palais Royal. Printing presses churned out radical papers. The price of bread rose, and in the worst riots yet seen in Paris an important manufacturer's house was burned to the ground. The King had had enough. For once he acted decisively and ordered troops into the city. The Assembly grew more and more uneasy as daily the number of troops in the city grew. They did not believe the King when he said that – following the riots – they were there to ensure their safety. Then on 12 July came the news that the King had dismissed Necker, his most popular minister. The people were furious. Violence broke out in Paris. Two days later a mob stormed the Bastille and let out the prisoners. That evening, 14 July, the liberal noble the duc de Rochefoucauld-Liancourt hurried to the King's private apartments at Versailles. Bowing over the King's hand, he told him the news.

"Is it a revolt?" the King asked him.

"No, sire, it is a revolution," the Duke is supposed to have said.

What must Louis have thought? Only a few months earlier he had held absolute power in France. Now that power was draining away from him. He appeared before the Assembly and assured them they had nothing to fear. He ordered the troops to be disbanded. He was still popular. It was the Queen who was disliked and blamed for any mistakes the King made. She who was accused of seeking to undermine the Revolution. She the cause of people's hunger. And when Artois, along with the princes of Condé and Conti, emigrated, their suspicions about her seemed to be justified.

In the countryside people's suspicions translated into fear. Rumours swept the countryside that enemies of France – both inside and outside the country – were plotting against them, and even that foreign troops had landed. People were terrified. Bands of peasants attacked châteaux, burning title deeds and feudal dues. This became known as "the Great Fear".

In Paris, deputies of the National Assembly – amongst them many nobles who had held office under the old regime – set about drawing up a new constitution to govern the country. No longer were Frenchmen to be subjected to the will of the monarch. They were to be free citizens, equal under the law. A Declaration of the Rights of Man and Citizen enshrined the right to free speech, to assemble and publish freely. All the trappings of privilege were to be swept away – titles, coats of arms, servants' livery. Aristocrats agreed to abolish their hereditary titles and what remained of feudalism was finally abolished. France's regions were to be divided into departments under uniform government. They made other changes too – seizing church lands to raise money, ending the payment of tithes to the Church, and compelling priests to accept a "Civil Constitution" and to sign an oath of loyalty to the state.

The King could not decide what to do. All that had seemed unassailable was being destroyed. He had been granted the right to veto legislation, but his attempts to do so often angered the people. In October 1789 he and his family had been forced to leave Versailles and live in the Tuileries Palace in Paris. He felt far from safe. What particularly upset him were the changes demanded of the Church. He signed the Civil Constitution of the clergy, but it made him very uneasy. He pretended to work with the Assembly but at the same time was secretly negotiating with foreign powers. One day, in 1791, when the King and Queen attempted to leave the palace to hear Mass at St Cloud, their coach was surrounded by angry crowds. In desperation, the royal family made a plan of escape. One night in June, their coach secretly left the palace. Travelling separately from the rest of the family the King's brother, the more moderate comte de Provence, escaped over the border. But the King was recognized and at Varennes his coach was stopped and the family were forced to return to Paris. Angry crowds lined their route. In Paris images of the King were smashed. People felt as if they had been betrayed.

The Assembly had also moved to Paris, and were housed in a hall near the palace. Following the King's attempted flight louder voices shouted for his removal. Moderate deputies joined radical members – known as Jacobins – in demanding the establishment of a republic. Foreign monarchs nervously followed events in France. The Queen's brother, Emperor Leopold of Austria, made an alliance with Prussia. But the move to war came from the French who felt threatened by the enemies that appeared to be surrounding them on all sides. When France finally declared war on Austria the King hoped he would soon be free. Early victories over the French reinforced that hope. But the tide turned and with it the King's fortunes. In the summer of 1792 voices warned that France's enemies would destroy the Revolution. People were rounded up – most of them innocent – and thrust into prison. In early September over 1,400 of them were murdered. These murders became known as the September Massacres.

Most of those aristocrats who had welcomed the Revolution now either left the country, or lay low on their country estates. The King was deposed and he and his family put in prison. A Republic was declared. In December 1792 the King was tried as an enemy of France by the National Convention – the fourth elected Assembly to govern France since the Revolution began – and in January found guilty and executed by guillotine.

The guillotine had been invented by Dr Guillotin as a more humane method of execution. It had first been used during the previous summer. But as fearfulness and suspicion grew in France and within the ruling body itself the number of executions began to increase. Guillotines were pulled into the centres of many towns where the inhabitants were known to be less than enthusiastic about the direction the Revolution was taking. Uprisings broke out in many parts of the country. Some wanted the monarchy to be restored, but many more were Republicans, concerned by the extreme radical measures that were being adopted by the government and calling for the constitution of 1791 to be reintroduced. War was being stepped up. France was at war with several European nations, including England.

In France everything that could remind people there had once been a monarchy was destroyed. Trees of Liberty were planted. A new Republican calendar was introduced. Towns and streets were given new names. Religious worship was forbidden. Churches were desecrated. In its place came the cult of Reason. Food was scarce. A cap – known as the Maximum – was placed on the price of food and other goods. Rationing and conscription were brought in. Revolutionary armies patrolled the countryside. Members of the Convention, called "representatives on mission", were sent into the regions to make sure that the Convention's policies were being adopted and that suspicious persons were arrested. Nearly everyone went in fear of arrest. The Law of Suspects, adopted in September 1793, made it possible to arrest people for the tiniest offence. The Terror, as this time was to become known, claimed many victims. There were not enough prisons to house all the suspects. Buildings like convents, monasteries and schools were speedily converted into prisons. It was not only the hated aristocrats that were imprisoned now – countless ordinary people were thrown into prison on the flimsiest of reasons. People were afraid to speak their minds. The streets were silent as few people dared to venture outside. Denunciations piled up on the desk of the public prosecutor, a man named Antoine Fouquier-Tinville.

The man behind many of these policies was Maximilien de Robespierre, the Jacobins' leader. The Jacobins had grown from being a moderate political club in the early days of the Revolution to a powerful body of radical men nicknamed "Montagnards" – after the high-tiered seats in the Assembly ("the Mountain") where they sat grouped together. Jacobin clubs had sprung up in towns across France. The Jacobins had defeated their more moderate opponents (the Girondins) in the Convention, and it was the most radical members of their party and their allies in the Paris Commune – the revolutionary local government of Paris – who now controlled the government. Robespierre had earned the nickname "the Incorruptible". What he longed for was a virtuous republic, a France reborn. But as time went on he was to become suspicious of everyone. Anyone who did not agree with his views must be an enemy of the reborn France. As the threat of invasion receded, other deputies called for the Terror to be brought to an end. But it was dangerous to oppose Robespierre. Those who did – even the most ardent revolutionaries like Georges Danton and Camille Desmoulins – found themselves walking up the steps to the guillotine on the place de la Revolution.

Finally, Robespierre's opponents judged they had enough support to bring about his downfall. Realizing that all was lost, Robespierre and some of his closest allies fled to the Town Hall. Hearing soldiers in the street below Robespierre attempted to take his life, but merely shot off his jaw. The next day he and his allies were pulled on a tumbrel through the streets to the guillotine while Parisians cried for joy. The Terror was at an end.

Members of the Convention began to examine prisoners' cases. Prisoners who had been expecting to die were now released. Jacobins feared for their lives as the "White Terror" was unleashed. In 1795 a new constitution was adopted and France was ruled by a government called the Directory. And a general who had made his name in the Revolutionary Wars was made commander-in-chief of the armies. In 1804 he would proclaim himself emperor. His name was Napoléon Bonaparte.

Timeline

1788 Riots in Grenoble. Some date this as the real beginning of the Revolution.

The Estates General ordered to meet by King Louis XVI.

"*Cahiers de Doléances*" (lists of grievances) are sent out to the people for them to state their complaints and concerns.

1789

April Hunger causes people in Paris to riot.

May The Estates General meets for the first time, after a grand opening ceremony in Versailles.

The Jacobin Club is formed. Its members are called Jacobins, after the old monastery on rue St Honoré in Paris where they meet. One of the most important Jacobins was Maximilien de Robespierre. Another important political club was the Cordeliers. Its members included Georges Jacques Danton.

June The Estates General declares itself the National Assembly and takes an oath (the "Tennis Court Oath") not to disband until it has drawn up a new constitution for France.

July National Guards formed throughout France.

The Bastille prison is stormed.

July–August The Great Fear.

August The National Assembly, which in July becomes known as the Constituent Assembly, abolishes the feudal system and adopts the "Declaration of the Rights of Man and Citizen".

October Women storm Versailles Palace. The King and his family are forced to move to Paris where they take up residence in the Tuileries Palace. The Assembly also moves to Paris, where it meets in a hall near the Tuileries.

November Church lands and property become the property of the state.

December France is reorganized into 83 departments, districts, cantons and communes.

The Treasury issues a new paper currency, called the "assignat".

1790

June Aristocratic titles are abolished.

July Paris's local government is reorganized.

The Civil Constitution of the Clergy is adopted, which subordinates Church to State.

1791

June The royal family attempts to flee France but is

recognized and brought back to Paris.

September A new constitution is adopted. The Constituent Assembly is dissolved and replaced by the Legislative Assembly.

Jews gain full citizenship.

Slavery is abolished in France, but not in its colonies.

1792

January–March Food prices rise. Riots in Paris.

April France declares war on Austria and Prussia.

June Crowds invade the Tuileries Palace. The red cap of liberty is stuck on the King's head and he is made to drink to the nation's health.

July The Duke of Brunswick, the commander of the Austro-Prussian army, issues a Manifesto, urging the French to rise against the Assembly, and promising reprisals if any harm comes to the King.

Mobilisation of French citizens.

National Guards enter Paris dressed in workmen's trousers and wearing red bonnets. People who dress this way earn themselves the nickname "sans-culottes". The patriotic song they sing becomes known as the "Marseillaise" (now the French national anthem).

Decree that the 'patrie' (country) is in danger. Émigré property is confiscated.

August A revolutionary Commune takes control of Paris.

The Tuileries Palace is stormed. The King's Swiss guards are murdered and the royal family imprisoned.

The Prussians, joined by French émigrés, invade France.

September The September Massacres.

The Legislative Assembly is dissolved and replaced by the National Convention.

The monarchy is abolished and a republic is proclaimed.

Divorce is legalized.

December The King is tried by the Convention as an enemy of the people and found guilty.

1793

January The King is guillotined.

February Food riots in Paris. France declares war on Great Britain and the Dutch Republic.

March Royalist (counter-revolutionary) uprising begins in the Vendée. It is eventually put down with great cruelty. It is followed later by uprisings against the Convention in other parts of the country, not all of them royalist.

Representatives from the Convention are sent into the provinces to ensure that the government's policies are being adopted. A Revolutionary Tribunal is set up in Paris to try political suspects. A Revolutionary Army is also created. Committees of Surveillance are established in local communes to investigate suspected enemies of the nation.

April A Committee of Public Safety is established. A Committee of General Security is also created.

Robespierre proposes a new 'Declaration of Rights of Man and Citizen'.

The revolutionary Jean-Paul Marat is put on trial by the moderate (Girondin) group in the Convention but is soon freed. (Later, the Girondins are themselves arrested and many of them guillotined.)

May A "Maximum" is decreed, limiting the price of bread.

July Marat is assassinated in his bath by Charlotte Corday, who is subsequently tried and guillotined.

August Metric system adopted in France. Universal conscription agreed.

September Riots in Paris. The "Law of Suspects" adopted, which ushers in the Terror.

Women required to wear the Revolution's tricolour cockade, which is already worn by men.

General Maximum on price of food and other goods.

October A new (Republican) calendar is decreed and adopted in November.

Queen Marie-Antoinette is tried and guillotined.

November Worship of God forbidden. In its place is the "Cult of Reason".

1794

February Slavery in France's colonies is abolished.

A law authorizes the seizure and redistribution of suspects' property.

April Danton and his allies are tried and guillotined.

May The cult of the Supreme Being is proclaimed.

June The Revolutionary Tribunal has its powers increased. This period is known as the Great Terror, when most executions took place.

July Robespierre and his allies are arrested and guillotined, ending the Terror.

August Prisoners begin to be released from prison.

November The Jacobin Club closes.

1795

February Freedom of worship is restored.

March The President of the Revolutionary Tribunal, Antoine Fouquier-Tinville, is tried and guillotined.

April–June The "White Terror". Royalists exact revenge on Jacobins.

June The Dauphin dies in prison.

August A constitution is adopted and the "Directory" is established. It rules France until 1799 when Napoléon Bonaparte proclaims himself 'First Consul' and declares that the Revolution is over. In 1804 he is crowned emperor.

The French republican calendar

The French republican calendar year starts in the month of September because that was when the Republic began. The calendar wasn't adopted until late November 1793, but was backdated to the date the Republic was declared – in September 1792. This is why the year from September 1793 is described as "Year II". Each month was 30 days long. The republican calendar was finally abolished in 1805.

1793–4

Vendémiaire (grape harvest): 22 September–21 October

Brumaire (foggy): 22 October–20 November

Frimaire (frost): 21 November–20 December

Nivôse (snowy): 21 December–19 January

Pluviôse (rainy): 20 January–18 February

Ventôse (windy): 19 February–20 March

Germinal (plant seeding): 21 March–19 April

Floréal (flowering): 20 April–19 May

Prairial (meadows): 20 May–18 June

Messidor (harvest): 19 June–18 July

Thermidor (heat): 19 July–17 August

Fructidor (fruit harvest): 18 August–21 September

Acknowledgements

My thanks go to Colin Jones, David Andress, Jo Daykin and Charles Palliser. I am particularly grateful to Graeme Fife for all his help and advice with this book.

Introducing...

My Royal Story

Vividly imagined accounts of queens and
princesses from the past.

Turn the page for an exclusive extract from
My Royal Story: Marie Antoinette
by Kathryn Lasky

January 1, 1769
Hofburg Palace, Vienna, Austria

I do solemnly promise to write in this diary given to me by my tutor, Abbé de Vermond, if not every day, at least every week, even though writing is not easy for me. For I shape my letters poorly and do not too often know the proper spelling. Still, this is my resolution for the new year.

Yours truly,

Archduchess Maria Antonia Josepha Johanna, daughter of Maria Theresa of Habsburg, Empress of the Holy Roman Empire of the Germanic Nations, and the late Emperor Francis of Lorraine

January 3, 1769

My second time writing. I am keeping the resolution. Abbé de Vermond would be proud. I spelled the word solemnly correctly, too, I think. I am grateful to the Abbé for giving me this beautiful little diary. It is blue, the colour of the sky, and has gold *fleurs de lis* engraved – the symbol of the French Court – or one of the many symbols. I must learn all the symbols of the French Court. I must learn French! Here now I shall list all the things I must learn over the next year:

· to write and read French (I speak it well, as it is the language of the Court here)
· gambling
· to dance in the French manner
· to walk, in the manner of the French Court, as if I float in the immense panniers, or side hoops, of the French ladies' dresses
· to read better
· to write better

Why must I learn these things better than other girls my age, better than any of my sisters or brothers, of which I have fifteen? Why? Because I am to be Queen of France. More about that later. My hand and my brain are too tired to explain.

January 4, 1769

I now am refreshed so I shall explain. I am just thirteen and before I become Queen, I must first be what the French call the *Dauphine*. It is their word for the highest Princess in the land. The Dauphine is the wife of the Dauphin, the eldest son of the King. The French King is Louis XV. His son died. So now his eldest grandson is the Dauphin. His name is Louis Auguste. I am to marry him, probably next year. And when Louis XV dies, the Dauphin shall become King Louis XVI and I shall become Queen Marie Antoinette. Together we shall rule. But for now I am an Archduchess. I am thirteen and everyone calls me Antonia. I am not yet ready to be a Dauphine, let alone a Queen. Everyone tells me this at least sixteen times a day.

Here is a list of the people who tell me this:

- Mama, the Empress
- Countess Lerchenfeld, my Grand Mistress, or governess. I call her Lulu for short.
- Noverre, my dance instructor

- Monsieur Larseneur, the French hairdresser
- Abbé de Vermond, the French tutor
- many brothers and sisters

I am not ready because I do not write or read in my own language well, not to mention French. Although I am a better reader than a writer, I just hate to read. But I am not stupid. I think some thought I was stupid. But Abbé de Vermond told Mama that I am "clever" and that I am "capable of learning and eager to please" but that I am a bit lazy. He gave me this diary because he thought that if I had someplace private to put my innermost thoughts, I would be more eager to write and thus improve my awful handwriting and spelling. He promises never to read it and, best of all, never to tell Mama I am keeping it. That is important because Mama is very nosy. *Extremely* nosy. I spelled that word, *extremely*, right. The Abbé would be very pleased but he shall never see it, if he keeps his promise. And I shall keep mine to him to keep writing. It does become easier each day. I think soon I shall write some more about my innermost thoughts. I'll make a list of the topics now for next time so I won't forget.

- Nosy Mama
- Caroline, my dearest sister
- My fat dead awful sister-in-law
- My favourite niece

January 5, 1769

This is fun. And Abbé de Vermond says I am improving in my writing and my reading. Already! And it has been only five days.

Now to my list.

1) Nosy Mama – I love the Empress my mother very much. But she and I are quite different. She is not so lazy as me. She never wastes a minute. Indeed, when she was in labour giving birth to me she called a dentist to come along with the midwife, for she decided to have an old rotten tooth pulled at the same time. She felt it was efficient to be in pain all at one time for two things. She is very orderly. Nothing is ever out of place. I misplace my handkerchief all the time and I lost my fan, the good one, that belonged to Brandy, my old governess whom Lulu replaced. Mama never forgets or misplaces things. But Mama is nosy. She wants to know everything I am doing, every bit I am learning. She tries to peek when I am getting dressed or undressed. She worries that my bosom might remain too flat, but with Caroline I remember her worrying that her bosom might be too large. "A heavy bosom adds

age to a young girl." That is one of Mama's sayings. She has many sayings, including the family motto, which she recites all the time. "Others make war, but thou, oh happy Austria, make marriages." These words are written in Latin on many crests and emblems around the palace. But that is not enough for Mama. She says it all the time – in Latin, in French, in German, and in Italian.

Mama's goal is to marry all of us children off to Kings or Queens, Princes or Princesses, Dukes or Duchesses. That is how the Empire grows, gets new land, and friends or allies to help us in times of war. Through marriage we can perhaps get peace. It is a very good bargain, in Mama's mind.

I think that is why Mama is so nosy. To make marriages, she must stick her nose into all of our businesses. So far she has done well. My sister Maria Christina married Albert of Saxony, and he is now governor of the Austrian Netherlands, the part we call Hungary. Maria Amalia married the Duke of Parma and is therefore a Duchess in Italy. My brother Joseph married fat Josepha of Bavaria, and my favourite sister Caroline was wed to Ferdinand, King of Naples.

Mama would be more nosy with us children if she had time, but because she is the Empress she is always working. Sometimes we go two weeks without seeing Mama. If someone were to ask me my very first memory of Mama, I would say it was when Brandy led me into her rooms of state at the summer palace, Schönbrunn, and Mama looked up from her papers. She had been peering at them through a large magnifying glass and she continued to hold it up and began to peer at me.

I had not intended to write this much. I am tired. My hand needs a rest. I shall find my brother Ferdinand and play shuttlecocks.

January 9, 1769

I am continuing my list concerning my innermost thoughts. Number two is Caroline. Do I say *is* or *was*? She is not dead but she is not here, either. It has been almost a year since I have seen her. Mama insisted that she marry Ferdinand of Naples. You see, my sister Josepha, who was older than Caroline, was supposed to marry him but Josepha died – the smallpox. So Mama insisted that Caroline "step in", as she put it. I loved Caroline dearly. She is three years older but we were very close. We were as close as … let me think … bees and honey or roses and thorns.

    chicks in a nest

    leaves to a twig

    bark to a tree trunk

You might think me nasty for saying this, but Caroline would be the first to agree. You see, I am considered quite pretty with my blue eyes and ash-blonde hair and very fair skin. Caroline is not. She is rather stumpy and very ruddy of face, prickly on the outside but lovely and beautiful inside. No matter, every rose must have its thorns – Caroline herself once explained this to me. And Caroline provided the thorns. She is fierce and independent, and she always protected me just as the thorns protect the rose from greedy people in a garden. She made an uproar when Mama insisted she marry the King of Naples. Mama said such an outburst was thoughtless and rude. But I loved Caroline with all my heart. She writes me, but it is not the same Caroline. She seems sad and almost weak in her letters.

I love my sister Elizabeth, too, but poor Elizabeth hardly comes out of her apartments. You see, Elizabeth was once a great beauty, really much more beautiful than I am, and very charming and witty, but she was stricken with smallpox. Her skin is deeply pitted. Elizabeth is twelve years older than I and she had been promised as a bride to the Duke of Bavaria, but of course it could not be, once her skin was ruined. She stays in her rooms now, heavily veiled, but at Schönbrunn in the summer she feels freer and wears thinner veils.

Before Caroline left for her marriage, I had really learned as much from her as from any of my governesses and maybe even more than from Abbé de Vermond.

Now number three on my list: Josepha, my sister-in-law.

No one liked Josepha, not even my brother who was married to her. Mama made him marry her. Josepha was miserable, cranky, ugly, selfish, and whiney. She caught the smallpox and died. No one was too sad. But Mama felt we had to pretend. She said we must appear to grieve. It was only proper. So she insisted that my older sister, who was by coincidence also named Josepha, visit her tomb. Well, the body was still warm in the coffin and the terrible pox must still have been alive in the air, because the very next day our dear sister came down ill and was dead within three days.

Josepha had been promised to Ferdinand of Naples as his wife. So that is when Mama insisted that Caroline take her place. So I lost two dear sisters just because of that miserable Josepha's death and, yes, Mama's notions about what is proper and a duty. God forgive me for these words but if I cannot help but think them, is it that much worse to write them down in this diary? And remember, God, I am writing this diary so that I might become a more learned person and fulfill Mama's wishes that I become Queen of France.

Enough! It makes me sad, and now the snow comes down thickly and we have been promised a sledge ride.

January 11, 1769

Today we went sledge riding and sledding. My dear little niece Theresa, or Titi as I call her, comes with us now that she is over her cold. She is just seven. She and I rode on the same sled. She rides stretched out on my back and we go whizzing down the slope. There are better slopes at Schönbrunn Palace out in the country. Here in Vienna there are not that many. It is too flat. But if we can get permission from the chief of the Imperial Guard, then Hans is allowed to take us across the river Danube to the other side where the Vienna woods slope down to the river. We then go to the Hermannskögel, which is the highest point in Vienna. We hope to go there tomorrow.

January 13, 1769

No time to write. Fresh snow and we have permission to go to the Hermannskögel. Titi and I are so excited!

January 14, 1769

No more sledge riding or sledding. Mama was furious when we returned the last time. First, I was late for my music lesson with Master Gluck. Mama came in to scold me for being late, as I had just begun on my scales. Mama takes our music education very seriously. She says we live in the centre of the best music in the entire world. For everyone knows that Vienna is where all the greatest musicians live and study and work. She even goes as far as to say that the music gets worse as soon as one leaves the city proper and keeps getting worse the farther one is from Vienna. She hates to think of what the music will be like in France, and in England, she cannot imagine.

In any case, when she came into the room, she lifted my hands from the harp. They were red from the cold, and she said, "Daughter! These are not the hands of an Archduchess, nor shall they ever be the hands of the Queen of France at this rate. You look like a scullery maid!"

She then ordered me to sleep in chicken-skin gloves. I hate more than anything those chicken-skin gloves. Even Lulu looked pained by the suggestion. It is an awful feeling, not to mention the odor of sleeping with chicken skin. But it is true that they whiten and soften the hands. Mama was so worried about Caroline's ruddy complexion that she had specially made for her a chicken-skin mask for sleeping that fitted over her eyes and cheeks. But Caroline took it off the moment she got in bed and the governesses weren't looking, and then the next day she would just powder her face more heavily. I wish I had Caroline's nerve in standing up to Mama sometimes. Except did it give Caroline what she wanted? She still had to marry that ugly old fellow from Naples.

January 19, 1769

Very boring days with no sledge driving. Monsieur Larseneur came today to work with my hair. They say that my forehead is too high and that my hairline is too far back. This is because Brandy, my old governess, used to always pull my hair back so tightly when I went to bed. It caused it to thin and break. Monsieur Larseneur is a fashionable Parisian *friseur*, as they call hairdressers in France. He does many of the Ladies-in-Waiting at the Court of Versailles. He is very friendly and we have nice chats. I learn how to spell many French words about hair from him. Here I'll make a list:

cheveux = hair

peigner = to comb one's hair

se coiffer = to do one's hair

se friser = to curl one's hair

épingle à cheveux = hairpin

You see, I am learning French. But I am bored. *J'ai beaucoup d'ennui.* That is French for "I have much boredom." I want to be sledge driving with my dog Schnitzel or my darling Titi.

January 20, 1769

Oh, I am so bored with the hair and the lessons and the dancing. But Lulu says they must get me near-perfect very soon, for a French painter is to make my portrait and then a miniature that will be sent to King Louis and the Dauphin. Mama feels if they see how pretty I really am it shall speed up the official engagement. You see, although this has all been planned since I was nine years old, it is not yet official, no date has been set, and that all depends on the French King. I wonder what the Dauphin looks like. Maybe they are trying to get him ready for a portrait. He is probably terribly handsome, as his grandfather the King is said to be the handsomest reigning monarch in Europe. I have heard that King Frederick the Great of Prussia is quite handsome but one dare not even whisper that name in front of Mama. Frederick is her great enemy. It is because of Frederick that we must all marry so well. Almost twenty years ago, just after Mama became Empress, Frederick invaded Silesia, part of our hereditary lands and our richest province. Mama never got over losing Silesia and vowed she would not sacrifice another centimetre to The Monster, as she calls King Frederick. She still vows to recover Silesia and we, her daughters and sons, are part of her plan. We lay siege not through weapons of destruction but through marriages.

So I must learn to dance. My hairline must grow back. I must improve my reading and writing and card playing. Card playing and gambling are favourite pastimes of the French Court of Versailles. All this is not so easy. I suppose marching and being shot at is harder, but not so boring.

January 23, 1769

Imagine this: while I practise walking with a book on my head to balance in the most immense panniers I have ever seen, which they tell me are quite the mode at Versailles,

Abbé de Vermond reads aloud to me the history of France. This of course was Mama's idea. "She can listen while she walks. She has ears as well as feet." Thank you, Mama. There is a special walk for the ladies of Versailles that has to be mastered. One must take very small, quick steps. This makes one's dress float over the polished marble floors.

January 30, 1769

Lulu tells me that Mama is very worried because King Louis has not yet sent a formal letter concerning my marriage. He apparently was supposed to do so by the end of this month. I always get worried when Mama gets worried, because she makes us, whichever child is worrying her the most, go with her to Papa's tomb at the church of the Capuchins to pray.

February 1, 1769

Guess where I was today – the Capuchins church with Mama. Oh, I just hate it. I was nine years old when Papa died, and

189

Mama has rarely worn anything but black since then. She cut her hair and she painted her apartments black. Now her hair has grown and her apartments are painted grey. But still the coffin she ordered made for herself at the time of Papa's death sits in the burial vault of the chapel beside Papa's, waiting for her. So Mama goes every afternoon and sits there beside the two coffins, the one with Papa's bones, the other empty, and prays. And today she brought me, too, to pray for my marriage, to pray for Silesia, to pray for good fortune against The Monster.